Russian Revenge

Russian Revenge
The Hoax at the Aqua

A Patti Mac Novel

NOLAN; SHAPIRO

Copyright © 2017 by Nolan; Shapiro.
Main cover and artwork provided by Christine Patchen

Library of Congress Control Number: 2016921171
ISBN: Hardcover   978-1-5245-7217-4
               Softcover   978-1-5245-7216-7
               eBook   978-1-5245-7215-0

All rights reserved. No part of this book may be reproduced or transmitted in any form or by any means, electronic or mechanical, including photocopying, recording, or by any information storage and retrieval system, without permission in writing from the copyright owner.

This is a work of fiction. Names, characters, places and incidents either are the product of the author's imagination or are used fictitiously, and any resemblance to any actual persons, living or dead, events, or locales is entirely coincidental.

Although the locales where this story takes place exist, various liberties have been taken, and this book does not purport to offer an exact depiction of any particular place or location.

Any people depicted in stock imagery provided by Thinkstock are models, and such images are being used for illustrative purposes only.
Certain stock imagery © Thinkstock.

Scripture quotations marked KJV are from the Holy Bible, King James Version (Authorized Version). First published in 1611. Quoted from the KJV Classic Reference Bible, Copyright © 1983 by The Zondervan Corporation.

Print information available on the last page.

Rev. date: 12/29/2016

To order additional copies of this book, contact:
Xlibris
1-888-795-4274
www.Xlibris.com
Orders@Xlibris.com
752571

CONTENTS

BOOK ONE

Chapter 1: Notification, May 16 3
Chapter 2: Saddle Up 7

BOOK TWO

Chapter 3: Long Beach City, One Month Earlier 11
Chapter 4: Comrades 14
Chapter 5: Once a KGB Man 16
Chapter 6: Target 19
Chapter 7: Weapon 21
Chapter 8: Motive 24
Chapter 9: Hatching the Plan 27
Chapter 10: Aqua Condominium 29
Chapter 11: Russian *Revansh*-Revenge 31
Chapter 12: Tanya and Grigori 33
Chapter 13: Death Sentence 36
Chapter 14: Launching Pad 38
Chapter 15: Pitch 40
Chapter 16: Negotiations 43
Chapter 17: Killenworth 45
Chapter 18: Isis Terrorist 48
Chapter 19: Arsenal 52
Chapter 20: Blindsided 54

BOOK THREE

Chapter 21: Board Meeting 61
Chapter 22: Smelling A Rat 64
Chapter 23: Moving to the Front Lines 66
Chapter 24: Operations Orders 70
Chapter 25: Closing the Deal 75
Chapter 26: Money Talks 79
Chapter 27: Muslims? 81
Chapter 28: Moving Day, May 14 83
Chapter 29: Weapons of Mass Destruction 85
Chapter 30: Martyrdom Video 88

BOOK FOUR

Chapter 31: Crime-Scene Investigation, May 16 93
Chapter 32: Exhumation 97
Chapter 33: Identification 100
Chapter 34: Crime Scene Number Two 103
Chapter 35: K-9 Dogs 106
Chapter 36: Search Warrant 110
Chapter 37: Peek First, Then Search 112
Chapter 38: Taking Down the Door 114
Chapter 39: Trace Evidence 117
Chapter 40: Command Post 119
Chapter 41: Media 122
Chapter 42: Joint Terrorism Task Force 124
Chapter 43: Antagonism Meets Defiance 127
Chapter 44: Karen 131
Chapter 45: FBI Supervisor Kelly Twomey 134
Chapter 46: Getting to Know You 137
Chapter 47: Tracking Grigori Glinka 141
Chapter 48: Russian Security Service FSB 144
Chapter 49: End of a Long Day 147

Chapter 50: Apartment 1-D 150
Chapter 51: Follow-Up 154

BOOK FIVE

Chapter 52: Roscoe, New York, July 5 159
Chapter 53: Double Cross 163
Chapter 54: Log Cabin 165
Chapter 55: Interrogation - George Hoffman AKA Yusuf
　　　　　　Al-Muslim 168
Chapter 56: Five Pillars of Islam 171
Chapter 57: Andrew O'Leary AKA Ahmed Yamin 174
Chapter 58: Tradecraft 177
Chapter 59: Skullduggery 180
Chapter 60: Cover-Up, July 6 183
Chapter 61: Coincidence, July 7 186
Chapter 62: The Director, July 7 189
Chapter 63: Make Something Happen, July 8 191
Chapter 64: Deliverance 194
Chapter 65: *Allahu Akbar* 197
Chapter 66: Posse 200
Chapter 67: Eye-in-the-Sky 203
Chapter 68: Party Crashers 206
Chapter 69: Combined Operations 209
Chapter 70: Follow that Bike 212
Chapter 71: Snafu 215
Chapter 72: Penthouse 218
Chapter 73: Hot Landing Zone 221

IN MEMORIAM

Russian Revenge is a novel about the ugly crime of terrorism. We dedicate this book to retired New York State police trooper Ronald G. Hoerner. Following police service, Ron took charge as the director of Security for Summit Security Services, Inc., at the World Trade Center. On September 11, 2001, Ron exemplified courage while rescuing a woman who was suffering from five broken ribs and a punctured lung. She had been traveling in an elevator when a terrorist-driven aircraft smashed into Tower Two.

Ron helped pull the victim to safety from the elevator shaft, turned her over to a security guard and a New York City EMT who carried the woman to an ambulance using a desktop counter as a makeshift stretcher. Within minutes of returning to his command post, Tower Two crumbled, leaving no trace of Ron Hoerner. However, his life was not given in vain. Although severely injured, the woman from the elevator survived.

Another remarkable event occurred in Ron's career. During his tenure as a state trooper, Ron single-handedly apprehended notorious Long Island serial killer Joel Rifkin. At the time of his arrest, Rifkin was transporting his latest murder victim, one of at least seventeen suspected cases.

* * * *

Greater love hath no man than this. That a man lay down his life for his friends.
                    -John, 15:13, King James Version

AUTHOR'S NOTE

We have relied on the use of patronymics regarding the widespread use of Russian middle names. The word *patronymic* literally means "father's name." The Russian patronymic is derived from the father's first name to identify the child. For example, the writer Tolstoy's name at birth was Leo Tolstoy. He was referred to as Leo "Nikolayovich" because his father's name was Nikolai.

It is considered polite to address a Russian named "Grigori Viktorovich" if his father's given name was Viktor, rather than just Grigori, which would sound rude.

BDS JFN

BOOK ONE

It is from the Bible that man learned cruelty, rapine, and murder, for the belief of a cruel God makes a cruel man.

Thomas Paine
The Age of Reason

CHAPTER ONE

NOTIFICATION

May 16

My friends call me Patti Mac. Subordinates call me Boss. The rest call me Lieutenant. Officially, my title is Detective Lieutenant Patricia Ann McAvoy, and for three years I have been the commanding officer of Nassau County's Homicide Squad South.

I had my hand on the doorknob when the infamous red phone rang. In homicide, the red phone means one thing, an eternal night has fallen on someone in Nassau County.

Temporarily alone, I had dispatched my squad to the parking lot of the adjacent police headquarters to celebrate Police Memorial Day. Cops all over the country bow their heads in tribute to fallen cops on May 15 of every year. This year, Memorial Day fell on Monday, the sixteenth. On my orders, the squad fell out to stand in the ranks, spit and polished, on parade.

The police department bagpipe band played the first chorus of *Amazing Grace*. I tend to shun ceremonies where *Amazing Grace* is played. The tune resurrects sad memories of my father's funeral mass. Chief Michael McAvoy was the legendary, unpopular head of Internal Affairs and served under three police commissioners.

Dad's motto, embedded in my DNA, was, "Always do the right thing because it's the right thing to do." Few of his colleagues showed up to bury him, and a chief told a reporter friend, "Of the dead, nothing but good should be said. I have nothing good to say except 'God damn Big Mac to hell and let the ground swallow him'." The reporter tipped me off. Slimy Deputy Chief Andrew Corcoran's name is in my book. Life is like a lazy Susan tray. What goes around comes around.

Mounted on a wooden shelf above the phone, the squad's mascot, a black ceramic vulture statuette nicknamed "first responder" stands guard. Ebony eyes stared as I cradled the phone in my left ear, lit a cigarette, positioned a yellow notepad, clicked my pen open and said, "Homicide South, Detective Lieutenant McAvoy here. Who's this?" hoping for a wrong number.

"Officer Tom Clark, Ninth Precinct, here. I'm at a boarded-up auto repair shop on Coventry Road in Westbury. My partner and I caught a 911 call for a burglary in progress. A neighbor saw three kids scale a gated fence and pry open a boarded-up window."

"Tom," I said, blowing smoke into the vulture's eyes, "how does this concern Homicide South?"

"A highway-patrol cop backed us up on the call. His partner is a cadaver-sniffing dog. By the time we got here, the burglars were in the wind and long gone, but—"

"Don't tell me. The dog is Caesar and he had nothing better to do but find a corpse?"

"How did you know, Lieutenant?"

"I've worked with Caesar, and his handler on a multiple-murder case in Long Beach. The eager little fellow sniffed out six bodies buried under the boardwalk."

"Oh yeah, I think I remember. Was that the case where the killers were assassinated at the courthouse?"

"Correct, Tom. Now, listen up. My troops are out of the office for the Police Memorial dog-and-pony show. I'm alone, and I have to round them up. We'll get out to you ASAP. Meantime, call out crime scene and emergency services. Use my name to get it done. I'll take care of the DA and the medical examiner. Stretch a band of yellow tape around the scene and for Christ's sake, don't touch anything."

"Understood, Lieutenant. There's one more thing."

In a murder investigation, I've learned there's never just one more thing. Information, evidence, clues, leads, and speculation come at you like waves breaking at a beach. Well-meaning sycophants tend to offer opinions. I keep my own counsel and tell them, "Thanks, but I don't need any more exercise by jumping to conclusions."

I hoped Tom had something significant to say. "Go ahead, Tom. Make my day."

"I shone my flashlight into the pried-open window. I'm pretty sure I saw a pool of blood and a couple of ejected bullet casings on the floor. I think I saw streaks of blood on the floor leading to the back door, like something or someone was dragged. Whatever Caesar found is outside the back door."

Ordinarily, I would have dismissed Tom's blood observation as an oil stain. However, cars don't leak shell casings. Now, it appears I'm to exhume a dead body carrying a few more orifices than God gave it.

"I'm on my way, Tom. If any reporters show up ahead of me, zip your lip."

"Reporters? They don't know anything about this."

"They scan our police radio traffic, Tom. They're like the vulture in my office, soaring around looking for a fresh kill. It's their livelihood, but I'll do the talking. We have a policy in this office: one voice, one voice only, and it's mine. One spokesperson prevents confusion and misinformation. Keep an eye peeled for the news choppers. They carry hi-tech cameras, sophisticated enough to spot a mouse in a cornfield. They might catch some of your mates smoking and laughing. You don't want to be singled out by the live-at-five news broadcasters. Give the troops a heads-up."

"Will do, Lieutenant. Thanks for the tip."

I hung up on Tom Clark who sounded like the kind of guy you'd hope for if you're in trouble and need a sharp cop. Remaining at the duty desk, I speed-dialed my sergeant.

CHAPTER TWO

Saddle Up

Detective Sergeant Frank DiGregorio picked up on the first ring as the last chorus of *Amazing Grace* drifted away. Of all the men who crossed my path in seventeen years of policing, Frank had emerged as one of a handful of trusted allies. He was approaching the mandatory retirement age of seventy, and every year, he announces, "This is it. I've paid my dues and I want to live to spend my pension." On our first homicide case, he took a bullet in the face and exposed our boss, Captain Brennan, as a corrupt cop. He survived the wound, and because of his courage to demolish the blue wall of silence, the captain was arrested. I was given a spot promotion and command of the Homicide Squad South.

"Frank," I said, "Gather Kowalsky, Horton, Cassidy, and Morgan. I want all of you to meet me on Coventry Road in Westbury."

I recited Officer Clark's report in detail and finished off with blood, shell casings, and drag marks. Frank got a rise from the tidbit. "Murder, most foul," he said. Great minds think alike. Frank was getting early dismissal from a memorial for the dead to meet and greet a new dead body.

I had a flashback to a popular television show filmed from a Las Vegas pawnshop. The owner, at the opening of each segment, says,

"Hey, I have learned one thing during twenty years in the business: You never know what's going to come through the door."

Homicide South's red phone is similar. You never know what kind of difficult case is going to pop out of the messenger of doom.

"Boss," Frank said, "should I call out the command-post bus?"

"Not yet, Frank. We'll follow protocol. Let's verify Caesar found a dead human and not the corpse of another dog."

"One more thing, Boss. The brass are eyeballing me. Should I say something?"

"No, Frank. I'll fill them in from the scene. Once they see you and the team getting in your cars, they'll be waiting for my call. Let 'em wait. Tell Kowalsky I took the call, but the case belongs to him. Saddle up."

Opening my desk, I retrieved my work shoes and dumped high heels into a tote bag. Heels, dirty yards, graves, and dead bodies don't mix. I slid on my flats, which were made for walking. I penciled "hold" in an open slot in the ledger and walked out the door to meet homicide number twenty-seven of 2016.

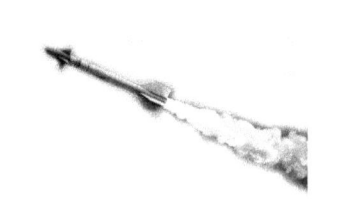

BOOK TWO

No trait is more justified than revenge in the right time and place.

Rabbi Meir Kahane
Never Again

CHAPTER THREE

Long Beach City

One Month Earlier

Pedaling his blue and white customized Trek bike, a man coasted along the resurrected Hurricane Sandy-demolished boardwalk. Long Beach City Fathers, fed by a smorgasbord of FEMA dollars, rebuilt a state-of-the-art boardwalk. Planks, laid in a diagonal pattern, met at a center lane running east to west like a backbone, restricted to bikers, joggers, and skaters. Bicycle-man spotted his bench-sitting friend lounging at a midway rendezvous point on one of seven-hundred-plus identical memorial benches erected following the Al-Qaeda 9/11 terrorist attack. Most of the World Trade Center victims were vaporized, yielding few dead bodies. With no grave to visit, families purchased benches, each adorned with a brass plaque, commemorating the life and death of a loved one.

Exactly 1.8 miles from the start of the boardwalk, bench-sitter waited on a tropical hardwood bench bolted to the boardwalk, under the Lincoln Boulevard light pole.

It was morning on April 15, Income Tax Day. Weather reports predicted an unseasonably mild, balmy day. Bicycle-man's friend, forty-four years old, was outfitted in expensive beachwear, a Tommy Bahama short-sleeve palm-tree shirt and tan shorts. A Panama hat matched his shorts. Ray-Ban aviator sunglasses masked his eyes. Birkenstock sandals, without socks, completed the outfit. A gold diamond encrusted Rolex watch and diamond ring decorated bench-sitter's left wrist and pinky. He had developed a middle-age belly with a forty-four-inch waistline to match his age.

A tern hovered on soft spring updrafts. Light gray upperparts, a black cap, and orange-red legs camouflaged his murder weapon: a narrow-pointed bill. Eyeballs alert for a reckless fish swimming near the surface. Precise as Robin Hood's arrow, the tern dive-bombed two feet under the water and speared his breakfast, which was nearly twice his size. The predator made off for the Lincoln Avenue jetty pursued by a posse of his fellow creatures, seagulls and terns. Arrow tern chomped on fish gut as he flew. Within seconds of landing and one more greedy mouthful, the rest of the tern's meal was torn apart amid the screaming and flapping of his pursuers' wings.

Bench-sitter watched the massacre in progress. The biggest of the gulls tried to gulp down fish remains. Nothing doing. Half the gull's size, the tern stood his ground and hacked into the gull's beak. Surrendering, the gull went aloft on the hunt for less adversarial prey like slow-moving crabs and clams.

Coasting alongside the bench-sitter, bicycle-man lowered his kickstand, waiting for a sign of recognition from his Russian comrade.

Bench-sitter never moved his head, gazing at the beach activity over the boardwalk rail. Wet-suited surfers paddled dangerously close to rock jetties. A daisy chain of cargo ships and oil tankers waited their turn for entry to the port of New York. First come, first served. Sand, taken over by lightly clad young mothers carrying blankets, coolers, pails, and shovels with preschool-aged children in tow were in abundance. Bikini-clad teens frolicked on the sand, tempting teenage hooky-playing boys, who hovered like the terns, hoping for whatever gifts the girls might bestow. Lincoln Avenue's section of Long Beach's ocean water is off-limits to all but the surfers guaranteeing safety for toddlers. Six-foot-long surfboards, propelled by waves, could mangle a child. Non-surfers understood the danger and either built sand castles or caught rays of the sun.

As the kickstand clicked into place, bench-sitter heard a voice from over his right shoulder. "*Dobraye ootro, tovarich,* good morning, comrade."

"*Zdrastvooyte,* hello, General Stankovich," Oleg Petrovsky said and smiled. Oleg's visitor's skin smelled of suntan oil, but his breath reeked of vodka. Without shifting his head, Oleg said, "I admire the surfers. They take risks and dare the rocks to do their worst. I'm here at your command, General. What do you want with me?"

CHAPTER FOUR

Comrades

General Mikhail Stankovich was a balding sixty-nine-year-old. Tufts of white curly hair jutted from his New York Mets baseball cap as he stepped between the guardrail and bench to face Oleg. Clad in a white V-neck shirt displaying a silver bicycle and chain, blue Docker cargo shorts, grungy sneakers and a backpack, the general was the opposite of Oleg in dress and physical stature. Tall and trim, he took a seat on the six-foot long composite bench forcing Oleg to face his visitor.

Oleg eyeballed the general's cadaverous face and thought, *I know you're near seventy, but you look beyond death.* With the smile and voice of a sycophant, exposing pearl-white teeth, Oleg said, "General Stankovich, it's been a long time since we worked together. You haven't changed since the Chechen wars. Bicycle riding has kept you trim."

Stankovich patted his stomach. "As you know, I've been a bike rider all my life. In 1972, I made the Munich Soviet Summer Olympics team. Duty called and I lost my only chance for a gold medal."

"*Da, tovarich,*" Oleg said and nodded to agree with his boss's visit to nostalgia land.

Stankovich ignored him. "I remember our first meeting after the Chechnya Islamic Brigade invaded their neighbor, Dagestan, to create an Islamic state governed by Sharia Law. We retaliated with brutal force. Chechen terrorists returned the brutality and waged war by placing car bombs in Russian cities, including Moscow. My brigade of KGB and *Spetsnaz* troops, including a very young Oleg Petrovsky, helped me eliminate hundreds of the Muslim zealots."

"I remember those days, General. The best years of my life. We did a great job for the *Rodina,* the Motherland. We recaptured Grozny and there was peace for a few years."

Passersby watched two men stand and embrace. Bear hugs and cheek kisses demonstrated the friendship the two Russian warriors had for each other. "For your information, Oleg Arturovich, the brave surfers hug the rocks on purpose. They allow themselves to get sucked out to the ocean by an undertow. They don't expend energy battling the breaking waves to make it to the spot where the waves crest. Surfers are smart. Look at the closed-circuit television camera near the Aqua's boardwalk. Surfers dial it up every morning to get a view of the breaking waves. On rare occasions, the ocean is calm, so they stay home. They know how to exploit their environment," Stankovich said.

"Then let's consider them both brave and smart, like us in Chechnya," Oleg said.

Stankovich smiled and said, "Oleg, your clothing testifies to an assimilation into the American culture. If I didn't know better, I would think of you as a Yankee tourist, or worse, a capitalist. You look like a forty-four-year-old stockbroker, rather than a veteran of the Federal Security Service. Your outfit makes us look like the prince and the pauper. You didn't dress like that in Chechnya. Russian KGB men don't dress like playboys."

"*Tovarich,* you haven't come to Long Beach to interview me for *Gentlemen's Quarterly,* have you? Your Soviet Union and the KGB is history. We now work for the Russian Federal Security Service. What's going on?"

CHAPTER FIVE

ONCE A KGB MAN . . .

Stankovich's pride was wounded. He stood over his subordinate and said, "Once a KGB man, always a KGB man. I've been ordered by the highest authorities in Moscow to oversee a mission of special importance."

Oleg clenched his right hand in a time-out gesture. "Wait a minute, General. 'Special Importance' is the highest security classification level. If this mission information is leaked, will it cause damage to the Russian Federation. Special Importance carries the same weight as the Americans' 'Top Secret' stamp."

"That's right, Oleg. Remember, our president Vladimir Putin was, and still is, a Soviet KGB man to his soul. He has read every available book on judo. He practices the art and knows how to take advantage of an enemy's weakness. He's the reason why no one back-talks to the Russians. Spectacular success is expected. I want you to help me run the operation."

"General, the plan sounds ominous."

"*Da, tovarich.* We have devised a master plan to rub the American Eagle's nose in dog shit. The *Rodina* will regain her place as a world superpower. Russia will emerge like a phoenix, rising from the flames of the bodies of Americans and Muslims."

Oleg removed his Panama hat, opened a handkerchief, and faced his former commander as he wiped beads of sweat from his brow. "That sounds like Russian poetry and, General, you aren't a poet. What's causing the Kremlin to wage aggressive actions on American soil? What do you mean by 'bodies of Americans and Muslims'?" Oleg the sycophant, became insubordinate. "Explain yourself. If you want my participation in the project, you'll have to give me details."

Stankovich clenched his jaw and thought, *You miserable tourist. I am a KGB general. I don't have to give details. You will follow orders and do what you're told or get a bullet in the back of your head KGB style.*

"As you know," Stankovich said in language softer than his thoughts, "I'm the proud son of a Red Army soldier. My father, Andre, fought the Nazis from Stalingrad to Berlin. Wounded several times, he survived the Great Patriotic War and received the Hero of the Soviet Union Medal of Valor for participating in placing the Soviet flag on Hitler's Reichstag. He indoctrinated me, his youngest son, and created a KGB cold-war soldier. My father's motherland trashed the Nazi fatherland and I'm prepared to devote our skills to humbling the American homeland."

"General, how can either of us, dedicated as we are, take on the American Eagle, the most powerful military machine on the planet?" Oleg asked.

Stankovich countered. "*Tovarich,* you're mistaken. The Americans have a powerful military machine manned by lions, but they're led by chickenshit donkeys afraid to use power. The Great American Eagle may fly high, but it feeds on rats and scraps. The Russian bear is king of the forest. Obama has scratched more red lines in the sand of the Middle East than there are oases in the deserts. Remember the words of Comrade Chairman Mao Zedong. He said, 'All power comes from the barrel of a gun.' Putin is cut from the chairman's bolt of cloth."

"What's the plan, General? Rhetoric doesn't make armies march. I want to hear the details," pushed Oleg.

Shifting his weight, Stankovich slung his arm over Oleg's shoulder. "I asked to meet you on this bench to reveal the target. Take your attention away from the young girls' asses, surfers, and terns for a moment. Lift your eyes."

CHAPTER SIX

TARGET

Oleg squinted through dark Ray-Bans. In the distance, streaking through buttermilk clouds, a blue and white Air France airbus descended parallel to the Long Beach shoreline, making for New York's John F. Kennedy Airport, a few miles to the west.

"Oleg, watch the pilot enter the glide path by raising the plane's nose, thrusting his engine and still descending. It's physics at work, defying gravity, quite remarkable. Every jumbo jet follows the same trajectory. An hour ago, the airbus was at thirty-three thousand feet clipping along at six hundred miles an hour. Now it's at two thousand feet lumbering at two hundred miles an hour. Flaps and landing gear down in what the pilots call dropping off the laundry. What was a sleek rocket has become a bloated elephant, locked into a landing pattern guided by a glide scope and air-traffic controllers. Planes keep to this pattern until they reach a position outside the airport. Then, following controller instructions, the pilot makes a dogleg right turn to the landing strip. It's nothing but a big fat fly waiting to be swatted," explained Stankovich.

"General, why are we swatting a jumbo jet? If operations and personnel rests solely with me, I need to know details, *tovarich*," pressed Oleg.

"Oleg, look over your left shoulder at the blue and white building. It's called the Aqua."

"I see it. Eight floors high. Looks new and expensive."

"*Da*, expensive. Each of three elevators is dedicated to just two units on each of the residential floors. Examine the wraparound balconies and penthouses overlooking the boardwalk, beach, and the airplanes."

Oleg's years of experience dealing with Russian intrigue had taught him his masters were capable of merciless actions. He counted the floors and balconies, watched a resident walk along the penthouse promenade, and looked back at the airbus.

"I begin to understand," Oleg said. "Your plan involves me and my team launching a heat-seeking missile from a balcony. How many passengers do jumbo jets like Air France carry?"

"Some transport four hundred souls including crew," answered Stankovich

Oleg sat silent, staring at the Air France plane, terns, and the seagulls. He pondered the mental image of voracious birds' beaks ripping away at the flesh and eyeballs of floating, dismembered dead bodies. *Neither terns nor gulls would give a damn if lunch was a man, a woman, or a child,* he thought.

"How is this possible, General? This isn't a hit-or-miss proposition. There's no margin for error. If my missile farts instead of exploding, the American army, navy, marines, and air force will be after us like a pride of lions on the hunt. What kind of missile will do this kind of work?"

CHAPTER SEVEN

WEAPON

Stankovich reached for his backpack and removed two manila folders, each crammed with photographs and diagrams. The general handed over a color photo of a ponderous rocket launcher, mounted atop a tracked vehicle. Four missiles arrayed in the launch position were locked onto a forty-five-degree angle.

"At first," Stankovich said, "I intended to use our Buk Gadfly missile launcher as shown in the photo. It's the same weapon we used to take down a Malaysian MH-17 passenger jet flying over eastern Ukraine last year. Buk is a formidable weapon but has flaws. For example, the Buk must be transported by a customized tracked vehicle the size of two tanks. A minimum of four soldiers, at least, are necessary to operate the tank and missiles. Loading and reloading takes up to twelve minutes. By that time, the passengers will land and clear JFK customs. It's too cumbersome for our mission. Camouflaged, the Buk would be perfect in a forest. Unfortunately, there's nothing here but blue sky, water, sand, and birds. I had to come up with something else."

"What's that, General?" asked Oleg.

"Open the other envelope, Oleg."

Ripping open the sealed envelope, Oleg dumped out another collection of color photographs and diagrams. Sitting silently, Oleg analyzed the pictures.

"This is a BB gun compared to the Buk. *Spaseeba,* please explain."

"You're looking at the Grinch. This 'BB gun', as you call it, can destroy an MIG fighter jet or an airbus. The Grinch is armed with one antiaircraft heat-seeking missile. Shoulder-fired, it weighs less than forty pounds, with a range of over six thousand four hundred yards and does the job, day or night," explained the general.

Aghast, Oleg stood, looked around to ensure no one was in earshot and said, "General, have you taken leave of your mind? The Grinch is etched with Russian markings and serial numbers. You can't fool the FBI forensics agents by sanding down the markings. They'll use acid to raise the numbers. Regardless, it's an easily identified Russian weapon. It'll be traced back to the *Rodina.* Why do this?"

"Besides André Stankovich, my other mentor is KGB General Aleksandr Sakhorovsky who preached, 'In today's world, where nuclear weapons have made military force obsolete, terrorism should become our main weapon'."

Oleg gripped the pictures, pored over them, and said, "General, this will turn Russia into a state sponsor of terrorism. I see a bearded young man holding a Grinch. He looks like an Arab. Who is he?"

"He's an ISIS-trained radical, now a key member of your team. He and his fellow ISIS gangsters made off with several Grinches from our arsenal at Tabqa airbase in Syria. We have recruited Mr. Andrew O'Leary to launch a Grinch missile from a penthouse courtyard of the Aqua."

Oleg shot a glance at the building. The magnitude of the crime hit him, causing a shudder in his shoulders. Trying to recover, Oleg said, "O'Leary? That's not Arab. Don't tell me. He's an American?"

"Not exactly, Oleg. O'Leary's mother, Fatima, is Pakistani, married to Henry O'Leary, an American. Henry taught tactics at the Pakistan Military Academy in Abbottabad, close to Osama bin Laden's hideaway. Following bin Laden's assassination, O'Leary's contract wasn't renewed, and the family emigrated to the US."

"So, what led Andrew to join ISIS?" wondered Oleg.

"O'Leary became an upper middle-class American Pakistani half-breed, or so he thought. Bored, looking for fame, he became radicalized in a local mosque. With our help, he went to Syria for ISIS terrorist training and returned to wage jihad on his adopted homeland. He's made to order and wants to meet Allah the moment he launches the Grinch. When the target is a fireball, Mr. O'Leary will be dispatched to paradise. The stolen Grinch and O'Leary will be found wrapped in the black ISIS flag. His martyrdom or suicide video shows him holding the Grinch over his head boasting that he stole it in Syria from the dumb Russians. After that, he can ascend to paradise to meet his harem of seventy-two virgins."

"What motivates a creature like O'Leary to wage war against his country?" Oleg said.

"O'Leary and his kind are losers. We search high and low for the O'Learys of this world who can be seduced, then we seduce them and turn them into our agents. O'Leary lived a good life, obtained a quality education but is a social outcast. He is a devout Muslim, attends mosque and prays five times a day. He has never shaken off the fact that he resides in a land hostile to Muslims. O'Leary, at twenty-five, has never held a job, lives in his parent's basement, plays video games, smokes pot, masturbates, and waited for a Fortune Five-hundred company representative to knock on his door. No one came, so he went looking for adventure and fame. It's an old story told by losers, 'I'll show them. I'll be somebody. I'll be a rock star'. Andrew O'Leary's face will be front page news, and everyone will be impressed. The American writer F. Scott Fitzgerald had a man like O'Leary in mind when he wrote, 'Show me a hero, and I will write you a tragedy'."

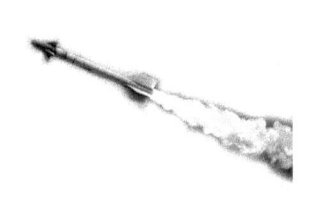

CHAPTER EIGHT

MOTIVE

"General," Oleg said, trying to change the subject. "Educate me. Other than what I see on the news, I don't know much about ISIS. I've made my living waging war with the Chechens. Is ISIS a danger to the national security of the *Rodina*?"

"*Da*, Oleg. ISIS is an acronym for Islamic State of Iraq and Syria and controls much of Iraq and Syria. They call the combined countries a caliphate. Four wars are being waged in the Middle East. Syria is in a life-and-death struggle between the government and rebels, another between Iraq and ISIS, three is a propaganda war involving Iran, Saudi Arabia and ISIS, and number four is a new cold war between Russia and America."

"I don't follow, General. Iran?" asked Oleg.

Stankovich rolled his eyes as if he were talking to a D-minus student. "Syrian President Bashar al-Assad is a key Vladimir Putin ally. In spite of this, America has armed and trained Syrian rebels. Now, many of those rebels are ISIS thugs, openly toting American made M-16 assault rifles. ISIS is on a mission to topple Assad. When that's accomplished, they want to incorporate Iran into their caliphate, something Putin is dead against. Putin is a fierce ally of Iran, and he wants Russian planes flying over Syria and Iranian military boots on the ground to rein in the caliphate. Syria's strategic importance places Putin in a position of relevance in the Middle East and access to a Mediterranean port. Putin is a big brother to Assad and wants to continue protecting him from Obama's empty threats recognizing that the *mullahs* are not a threat to regional security, but that Washington and ISIS are."

"I begin to understand, General."

"*Da*. America is using ISIS as a surrogate to attack its enemies in the Middle East, to serve as camouflage for U.S. military intervention abroad and at home to foment a manufactured domestic threat. The so-called War on Terror is a pretext for maintaining an oversized military. Is that sufficient, Oleg?"

"So, General, your strategy is to ensure ISIS takes the blame for destroying a jumbo jet on American soil or, to be more accurate, over American water?"

"*Da*. America is a nation of cowboys, quick to shoot first and ask questions later. They govern by polls and focus groups. Following nine-eleven they rushed the Patriot Act through Congress in forty-eight hours, likewise for Pearl Harbor. The U.S. Congress declared war on Japan in less than thirty-two hours. Terrorism incites the American public to demand a heavy-handed response."

"What kind of response, General?" inquired Oleg.

"Your actions will infuriate the Americans. They'll declare a formal state of war between ISIS and the United States. America will invade the ISIS caliphate in Iraq and Syria, Libya, Yemen, and anyplace where the black flag of ISIS flies. Predator drones, hellfire missiles, stealth bombers, the Second Marine Division, Eighty-first Airborne Division, and every SEAL unit will run amok slaughtering ISIS radicals. Meantime, Putin will gain breathing room to bolster the Assad regime in Syria. As the American onslaught continues, Moscow will emerge as the premier protector of Iran, Syria, Saudi Arabia, Iraq,

Kuwait, Bahrain, Qatar, and billions of oil barrels percolating under the sand."

Oleg stood up, stared into the rigid face of a cold war KGB general.

"General," he said, "what's driving you to participate in this atrocity? Your actions will start World War III."

CHAPTER NINE

Hatching the Plan

"Oleg,' Stankovich began, "long before I met you, I was an operative in Afghanistan, serving the *Rodina* with my beloved brother, Yuri. The war was going well until the American CIA covertly supplied stinger missiles to the mujahedin. One of those stingers killed my brother, a hind-attack helicopter pilot. I want the Americans to grieve as I have grieved. I hate America and all things American. I also have discovered the name of Yuri's killer, a Muslim holy warrior, who's going to meet Allah when this mission is completed."

Stankovich rose and went nose-to-nose with Petrovsky. "Read the name etched into the brass memorial plaque on the back of your bench."

Oleg looked down and read the plaque. He had received orders to wait at this bench and was embarrassed for not spotting the name the moment he sat down.

Yuri Andre Stankovich
Murdered in 1986
A Hero's Death

Stankovich nodded. "That's right, my beloved brother, Yuri. Those damned stingers signaled the beginning of the end for the Soviet Union in Afghanistan. The loss of Afghanistan led to the breakup of our empire. I will never forget. Now it's time for *revansh*—revenge. I think the plan is brilliant. It has few moving parts, and the *Rodina* will walk away with her chastity intact."

"What's next, General? How do I help? When do we begin?"

"You will stroll along the boardwalk to the Allegria Hotel. At eleven a.m., wait for a ride near the entrance lobby. Grigori and Tanya will be driving a green Range Rover to chauffeur you."

"Grigori and Tanya? Are they here? I thought they were in Moscow for special training courses. They kept their movements secret even though they've been assigned to me. How can I trust people who don't keep me informed?" demanded Oleg.

"Their mission was on a need-to-know basis. Your people were on a mission of Special Importance to Turkey and Syria. Now you know. Stop bellyaching, Oleg. It's unbecoming for a Federal Security Officer. Your team returned incognito to the U.S. by way of Mexico. They crossed the border at Tijuana carrying legitimate-looking passports with no questions asked. For your information, ISIS has seized a Syrian passport control center and prints perfect passports for a hefty fee. They can't be considered forgeries, since they are the real thing. ISIS plans to flood the U.S. with jihadists like O'Leary. We want to be ahead of the ISIS terrorist attacks to come. ISIS radicals will be arriving later this year. Most will be acting as lone wolves. The body count will be enormous. There is no border security in this country," asserted Stankovich.

"Where am I going in this Range Rover, Mikhail?" inquired Oleg.

"To meet your ISIS assassin, O'Leary. Before I disappear, there are several things I want you to know."

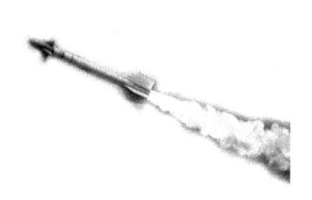

CHAPTER TEN

Aqua Condominium

With a tilt of his head, General Stankovich motioned to the Aqua Condominium, a modern oblong structure, the opposite of the boxy 1950s architecture of the surrounding buildings. Realtors list the Aqua as the most upscale oceanfront condo in the tristate area, a premier piece of Long Beach real estate. Each Aqua unit is outfitted with three wrap around one-thousand-square-foot balconies. Decorated in striking blue paint, blue tinted glass, offset by an off-white background, the building sits astride the boardwalk and the Atlantic Ocean like a moored cruise ship.

"Your agents, Grigori and Tanya, will meet the board president, Jules Goldberg. He has been told there is legitimate interest in buying three condominiums."

"Why three? Wouldn't one meet our needs?" Oleg said.

"One and three are on the penthouse level from which the missile will be launched. Number two is located the floor below the penthouse. We'll own the top and bottom, leaving our back covered."

"Good military tactic, General, covering your flanks. You are indeed the son of a soldier. What time is the meeting?"

"It's set for ten o'clock. Neither of us will be there. Tanya, posing as a real estate broker, and Grigori as the buyer, will represent us. Grigori is supposedly an agent for his Russian father. I don't want anyone to see our faces. Tanya and Grigori are expendable. We are not."

Agitated and upset about being kept out of the loop, Oleg raised his voice to scold the general. "Tanya and Grigori? I don't trust them. How can I when they have shown such disloyalty?"

"Trust is not an issue, Oleg Arturovich. I handpicked them from all our agents on American soil. Tanya and Grigori are devoted soldiers and know how to obey orders. I served with their fathers in the glory days of the Soviet Union in Afghanistan. Their fathers were *Komitet* men from their foreheads to the tip of their toes. The men passed KGB DNA into the genes of Tanya and Grigori. Graduates of the FSB Academy, they were secretly recruited months ago and sent on an overseas mission of Special Importance. The mission included recruiting Andrew O'Leary."

Oleg muttered, "General, I have many questions. How do I know this mission has been authorized by the highest authorities? I mean no offense, but you have a reputation for going your own way, on the prowl for medals and promotions. I have no way of verifying the authenticity of the orders."

"Oleg, *vyso mogu* I can do anything." The presidium of the Soviet Union is backing me.

Oleg shuddered as he began to understand. *Oh my God. Presidium? It was abolished in 1991 after Boris Yeltsin took power. Stankovich has become a megalomaniac. He's making this up, living a delusion to get even for his brother. Watch yourself,* he thought. Treading carefully, Oleg posed his next question.

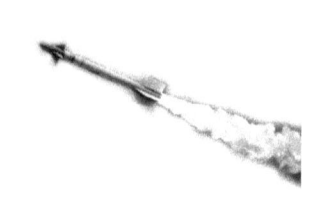

CHAPTER ELEVEN

RUSSIAN *REVANSH-* REVENGE

"What have your real estate broker and buyer accomplished to bring them to this level of trust?" asked Oleg.

"They successfully recruited and sent the ISIS shithead Andrew O'Leary to Syria for training. O'Leary believes Tanya and Grigori are also Muslim and ISIS sympathizers. After a weekend in bed, Tanya prompted O'Leary to pose for his martyrdom video. She wrote the script, and the idiot spouted every word into the camera, introducing himself as a *shahid*, or martyr. She scrupulously avoided using the word *suicide* because the act of self-destruction is a great sin forbidden by the Koran. O'Leary has changed his American name to Ahmed Yamin at Tanya's urging," said the general.

"What the hell did she say to induce him to recite the speech, General?" asked Oleg.

"She earned his trust. Anticipating a challenge from O'Leary regarding her knowledge of Islam, she was ready for a religious interrogation. She described a pilgrimage to Mecca where she prayed before the Kaaba, a building covered with a clean black silk cover, embroidered in contrasting golden threads. Kaaba translates to 'cube' in Arabic. Tanya also vowed to travel with him to Paradise and live for eternity as one of his concubines. Tanya and Grigori have convinced the assassin they are Muslim zealots from Chechnya. During their orientation, I sent them for Islamic religious training. They were proficient enough to make the annual *hajj* pilgrimage to Mecca and pass a religious interrogation. Both are now known in the Muslim world as *Hajj* Grigori and *Hajj* Tanya. She's primed to eliminate O'Leary as soon as his finger leaves the Grinch's launch button. You may have faith in our agents. I certainly do," asserted the general.

"You're scaring me, General. Sounds like anyone who gets in the way of General Mikhail Andreovich Stankovich may never be seen again. Does the operation have a code name?"

"Of course. It's been named Operation *Revansh* for revenge. The code name was issued in honor of my brother, Yuri," Mikhail said, as he embraced his friend. "Oleg Arturovich, of all people, you have nothing to fear. You're my point man and ATM machine for Tanya and Grigori. Russian *Revansh* won't work without passing around many envelopes stuffed with cash. The Aqua units are owned by yids, and yids love money."

Oleg rose from the bench and leaned over the guard rail. Facing the ocean, his peripheral vision picked up another plane flying in from Europe to JFK Airport, a Delta Airlines jumbo jet. "I see the Delta pilot is dropping off his laundry," Oleg said as the landing gear and flaps came down.

He continued, "Will that beast go down with one shot, General? I have deep concerns about mass murdering hundreds of civilians. If we get caught, we'll be considered worse than ISIS and hunted like Nazi war criminals. I have a sense of foreboding. All I will get out of this adventure is a cyanide needle buried into my arm in a U.S. federal prison. Swear to me on the sacred *Rodina* this thing has to be done."

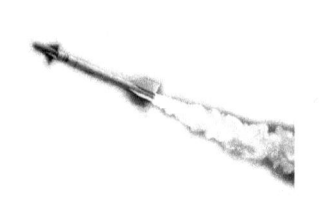

CHAPTER TWELVE

TANYA AND GRIGORI

"Oleg, Russian *Revansh* orders come straight from the Kremlin. An incoming or outgoing aircraft will be gone with less effort than it takes for you to flick away a cigarette butt. Before I swear an oath on the *Rodina*, I want to reveal the background story of an act of terror leading to this mission. Putin has been in a rage with the Chechens since September 1, 2004," said Stankovich.

"I'm not connecting the date, General. What did the Chechens do?" Oleg said.

"An act of barbarism to make the Nazi hordes look like choirboys. Thirty-two terrorists invaded Beslan School Number One on the first day of class. For three days, they held twelve hundred men, women, and children hostage forcing them to drink urine and eat flowers. When it ended, three hundred thirty-one people were dead, including one hundred seventy-six children."

"Why so many adults in an elementary school, General?"

"On the first day of class, it's customary for parents and grandparents to accompany the little ones to school. They call it the 'Day of Knowledge.' The children bring gifts and flowers for the teachers. Unfortunately, the flowers wound up in the children's stomachs. Putin has called Beslan Russia's nine-eleven, and he is hellbent on making the

Chechens pay. While the world's attention is focused on the American invasion of the caliphate, Putin is going to clean house in Chechnya. Now, I will show you my sincerity."

General Stankovich rose and lifted his T-shirt revealing a full chest tattoo of a woman dressed in a white robe, carrying a silver shield in her left hand, and brandishing a sword in her raised right hand—the universal symbol of Mother Russia, the *Rodina*. Stankovich placed his right hand over the tattoo and said, "I swear this to you on the sacred *Rodina* and my honor as a KGB officer. Taking down an airline has to be done."

Oleg stared at the tattoo, heard the general's oath and thought, *He's gone over the edge. He believes every word. I have to get out of this madness.*

Stankovich smiled. "Do you believe me now, Oleg?"

Oleg nodded his head. "*Da*, General, I believe you and will follow your orders."

"Not my orders, Oleg. Moscow's orders."

Stankovich mounted his Trek and headed for a clandestine meeting with Grigori and Tanya before the real-estate mission. As he made his way to a boardwalk exit ramp at Lincoln Boulevard, Stankovich walked his bike down the ramp, following instructions posted on a sign. *Don't attract attention*, he thought.

"*Paca*, Oleg, good-bye," Stankovich yelled over his shoulder, thinking *you have become a soft American donkey. There's no room in this mission for a weak sister. Yes, indeed, you will soon get the more formal Russian good-bye. Das Sveedaneeya, Oleg.*

Pedaling to Park Avenue, Stankovich found Tanya and Grigori sitting in a Range Rover in the parking lot of a Catholic church, Our Lady by the Sea. They left the car and walked to a coffee shop. Grigori, a handsome black haired thirty-year-old deferred to his slightly older partner Tanya. "Walk with me," Stankovich said. "I have something to tell both of you."

On the way to a coffee shop, Stankovich walked his bicycle. Tanya and Grigori flanked him like a pair of bookends, hanging on every word.

Stankovich began, "Comrades, you're too young to know the details of what I am about to say. I have lived through desperate times for our country. That is about to end. We are opening the front door to Cold War Two. Cold War One was held in check by the concept of Mutually Assured Destruction, known as MAD. Our Russian Federation now has the military power to dwarf MAD. Two historical events happened at the end of 1999 and 2000. First, President Clinton used NATO to bomb Belgrade and destroy Serbia. NATO emerged as the real threat to Russia because the Warsaw Pact had dissolved. The Russian bear lost his teeth and fangs. Second, in 2000, President Vladimir Putin took over and vowed to make Russia great again. Our plan, with his complete support, is to goad the United States into formally declaring war on ISIS. Your mission is to provide the means for the declaration of war. We believe the NATO countries will back off, in spite of their infamous Article Five—an attack on one nation is an attack on all. Because of Russia's overwhelming strength, NATO will fade into a footnote in history lessons."

Grigori, walking alongside his general, said, "This is an historical undertaking. We won't fail the *Rodina*."

"There is one more thing, Grigori. Use your skills to evaluate the commitment of Oleg to the mission. I leave it to your judgment. He's either with us or he's against us. Enjoy your coffee. Make sure you take his car keys, if you decide he's not with us. Pick up Oleg at eleven o'clock. Remember, I depend on you."

General Stankovich mounted his bicycle, swallowed a swig of bottled water, and rode along Park Avenue disappearing over the Long Beach Bridge.

CHAPTER THIRTEEN

DEATH SENTENCE

Jules Goldberg, Aqua board president, paced on the penthouse atrium of unit 805 with the owner, Marvin Taub. Jules, a retired stockbroker and avid golfer, was dressed in a blue and white striped Callaway shirt with white shorts and sandals. Nearing sixty, he depended on large Coke-bottle glass spectacles. Taub was anxious. His anxiety was generated by his ex-wife suing him for back alimony in the amount of a quarter-million dollars. He had a lot to gain. Unloading his apartment meant he could convert the sale into cash and fade into oblivion, leaving an ex-wife to live on food stamps. Front desk security had notified Taub that two visitors were arriving by private elevator.

Aboard the private elevator, Grigori said to Tanya, "General Stankovich has trepidations about Oleg's commitment. The general said, 'a lifetime of circling enemies has filled me with an encyclopedia of knowledge for reading body language. I fear Oleg has been Americanized, wearing expensive clothes, dining at Manhattan's Palm Restaurant with his girlfriend, Karen, drinking Blue Label scotch. She's eight years younger than Oleg and plays the violin for a symphony orchestra'. I, rather, we are authorized to make an evaluation of Oleg's commitment later today. The decision to retain or eliminate Oleg is ours. The general will support us either way."

"Grigori," Tanya said. "I heard the conversation and the tone of Stankovich's voice. Sometimes you can be so naive. He told you to take his car keys. That means Oleg isn't going home today, or any other day for that matter. Men like the general rarely give direct orders. Stankovich didn't achieve his rank by observing the Marquis of Queensbury rules. He's a ruthless, merciless killer. His suggestion to leave the decision to whack Oleg is his way of testing us. If Oleg gets off the hook, then balks and causes a problem, we will suffer the consequences. Visitors wearing shabby black suits will come to our apartment, and they won't be stopping by for shots of vodka. When we get back to the car, dig your Glock out of the car's secret compartment. Load the magazine and slide a round into the chamber. We may not have time for anything but a clean shot. General Stankovich is afraid our Oleg may get swallowed up in the labyrinth of lost souls—the American Federal Witness Protection Program. Grigori, do you want me to do it, or will you?"

"I'll do it, Tanya. He gave me the orders. You're right. It's a test," Grigori said, his face turning crimson, like he had spent the day in the sun.

"Good. I'll distract him. I've caught Oleg looking at my backside while ignoring everything around him. At that moment, take him out, Grigori."

Grigori looked his partner up and down and let his eyes rest on Tanya's buttocks. Pointing to them, he said, "That will be the last thing Oleg will ever see."

CHAPTER FOURTEEN
Launching Pad

Taub, junior to Jules by ten years, left the penthouse door ajar and returned to his terrace, wanting to make a visual appraisal of the agent and buyer. He and Jules were caught off-balance by the Russian broker's attractiveness.

Tanya, a thirty-year-old raven-haired beauty sauntered into the apartment foyer. Taub's eyes swallowed her. In a black pencil skirt, white blouse, and black patent leather stilettos, she was a sight to behold. Matching her heels, a Michael Kors bag dangled from Tanya's left shoulder. Her ensemble was set off by a white pearl necklace. Metal heel taps announced to the terrace boys, *look out, Tanya is here*. Trailing behind, Grigori was overshadowed by his glamorous partner.

Tanya, well trained in secret-service machinations, scanned the large apartment from the foyer. Two original Pablo Picasso paintings hung from ten-foot-high living room walls. The dining room and kitchen were installed with stainless steel Viking brand commercial appliances and a marble dining table. Moving along, she observed a rolling bar, fully stocked with expensive liquor—Johnny Walker Platinum Label and an unopened bottle of fifty-year-old Glenfiddich. Wine bottles bore labels telling her each cost more than a hundred dollars. *Windows everywhere*, she thought. *Too many windows*. Then her trained eye saw hidden shades to be raised or lowered by remote control.

Taub switched his eyes from Tanya to Grigori, and he whispered to Jules, "He's very young to be parading around with the kind of cash to pull off this deal. I want three million dollars for my penthouse. Not one penny less. If either he or the pretty Russian czarina haggles with me, I'll throw them out."

"You crook," Goldberg said. "I happen to know you picked up the unit last year for one point eight million dollars."

"So, goyim money is as good as the next guy's. I want what I want."

Buyer and seller met on a wraparound balcony and were escorted to the penthouse rooftop deck. Tanya noted a collection of rich boy's toys including a hot tub, silver Genesis Weber BBQ grille, wet bar, bathroom, and arbor. An ample supply of chairs and chaise lounges scattered about the area could accommodate fifty guests, bartenders, and waiters. A DJ would easily fit into the floor plan. Tanya took in the vista from horizon to horizon. She picked up on the sights Oleg had witnessed from his bench, only this time from eighty feet above the ocean. Surfers, jetties, terns, hooky-playing teenagers, and mothers at their wits' end trailing after out-of-control tots were barely identifiable.

An apartment house box-style building on Lincoln Avenue, opposite the Aqua, rose to six stories, at least twenty feet lower than the penthouse.

Perfect, she thought. *We could take down a plane with a slingshot from this height and distance. The arbor and three-foot-high parapet will mask O'Leary until he's ready to fire.*

CHAPTER FIFTEEN

PITCH

Tanya extended her hand, made introductions, and handed out her business card. Tanya Dubov, Realtor. Goldberg stepped away for a shot of Johnny Walker. "Money negotiations are none of my business," he said.

"Please stay, Jules. We would like you to hear this," Tanya said.

Jules, Tanya, Marvin, and Grigori sat on spacious Woodward rattan furniture. Colored gray, with off-white plush pillows, they resembled lounge furniture found on cruise ships designed for luxurious comfort. Taub offered to make cocktails and offered small talk. "So, where do you folks come from? You don't seem to have a Russian accent."

"We were born in Grozny, the capital of Chechnya," Tanya said. "Our families moved to Moscow when we were young to attend private schools, taught by English-speaking instructors. We learned English as a primary language and lost our Russian accents, as you call them, before our speech patterns were formed."

Tanya then shook her head at Taub's offer of cocktails. "I never drink when I'm working, Mr. Taub. Besides, it's not five o'clock," she said, glancing at her black-and-silver Movado watch.

Grigori spoke, "I represent my father who has given me full power of attorney to negotiate the deal during his absence. In addition to the three apartments, Father has special needs."

Taub and Goldberg blurted out the same question. "What special needs?"

Grigori unfolded a sheet of paper from his suit pocket. Reading aloud from a typed list, he said, "Bullet-proof glass on all windows, steel doors on all entry points, and shockproof titanium on the walls, floors, and ceilings. The elevators must be modified to bring them up to a secure status. That means armor plating and a high-speed lift motor. Fobs must be replaced with eye- and hand-recognition technology. He also wants a helicopter landing pad on the roof."

Grigori paused as he took note of Goldberg and Taub exchanging glances.

"We will replace your unarmed guards with *Spetsnaz*-trained security throughout the building. They're Mother Russia's men of steel, real pit bulls. One for concierge, and a roving guard. We'll house them in one of the apartments. Each man is a licensed pistol holder and has over a decade of experience. They'll work an eight-hour tour-of-duty with appropriate break periods."

Taub didn't blink. Goldberg shifted his weight. He was nervous. His tongue was looking for a taste of scotch whiskey. This was out of Goldberg's league, and Taub knew it. Taub examined the body language and persona of Grigori who was about thirty, well dressed in a blue business suit, white shirt, red tie, and articulate. His black shoes shone like a waxed Cadillac in a showroom.

"OK, Grigori," Taub said. "I get it. Your father is one of Vladimir Putin's oligarchs and money is no object. Jules and I need to know why all the security is necessary."

Goldberg nodded his head, afraid to ask the question, or rather afraid of the answer.

"Well," Grigori said, "my father is a multinational businessman and security is for the protection of his visitors. Dad will be in residence for six to eight weeks annually. We will use separate apartments for his guests, which will include my grandmother and foreign dignitaries."

"What type of dignitaries?" Taub said.

"The Israeli ambassador to the United Nations, King Abdullah of Jordan, prime minister of England, and other notable politicians."

Tanya chimed in. "Mr. Taub, would you like to speak to Grigori's father who is in India?"

CHAPTER SIXTEEN

NEGOTIATIONS

Before he could answer, Goldberg said, "Not now, Tanya, the modifications being requested can't be discussed without speaking to the other board members. I'll have to do some research on what's involved or even allowed. Your client wants to purchase oceanfront apartment 705, and penthouses 805 and 806, correct?"

Taub sat silent, cursing himself for not asking for ten million dollars. *This Grigori has access to Cayman Islands bank account money,* he thought. *Three million is chump change.*

"Yes, Jules," Tanya said. "The amount settled upon will be paid in cash. No need for mortgages in this transaction. Perhaps you should work up a price for buying the entire building," she added, half joking.

"OK, Tanya. I'll convene a board meeting and get back to you as to how or even if we may proceed. A helicopter pad on the roof is unlikely from a structural standpoint and Long Beach City residential building codes," Jules said.

"Oh well," Grigori said, "Father has already landed a chopper on the beach in front of the Allegria Hotel."

"Grigori," Taub said. "My selling price for this unit is set at four million dollars and that's not negotiable. Improvements, updates in security are on your dime. Understood?"

"Understood, Mr. Taub. We'll fund an escrow account from which the Aqua may draw from for payment of our upgrades, especially the armed security force."

Grigori stood and walked to the balcony rail. Staring at the blue sky, he said, "Mr. Taub, my father might be concerned about noise from jet aircraft. On the way here this morning, I noticed several jumbo jets flying low heading toward JFK Airport. Do they fly close enough to the Aqua to make a lot of noise?"

"Ah, Grigori," Taub said, glad to get this problem off the table. "The jets parallel the coast of Long Beach in their landing patterns and are high enough to muffle the engine noise. They don't fly out of JFK until after five p.m. It's all part of noise abatement regulations. They're also high enough to drown out the engine noise. There are a number of flights heading to Europe in the early evening hours. They travel at night in order to land on the continent in the early morning. There's one exception to the night flights."

"What is that, Mr. Taub?"

"El Al doesn't fly on Friday nights. Jewish Sabbath, you know. Jewish law prohibits work of any kind from sundown Friday to sundown Saturday. The other carriers are not affected."

CHAPTER SEVENTEEN

KILLENWORTH

Tanya hooked up her seat belt, paused before clicking it, and said, "Grigori, you showed initiative. Asking the question about the airplane noise was an intelligence coup. We might have spent days trying to analyze the plane logistics. You went ahead and got the answer. Daytime launch of the missile is out of the question. I'd like to launch the Grinch at night. The weapon is equipped with a passive infrared homing device and night vision. Our people built in the 'fire and forget' concept. One shot, one kill. Let's go pick up, Oleg, the reluctant warrior."

They found Oleg waiting in front of the Allegria, a five-star hotel. Parked on the street, Oleg sat in a new BMW sporting New Jersey license plates. Oleg looked pensive.

"There he is, Grigori. Parked on the street, acting like a caged panther, darting his head back and forth. Our Oleg seems lost. Beep the horn so he can find us," Tanya said.

Oleg glared at the Range Rover. *Who do these bastards think they are?* he thought. *They work for me and beep the horn like I'm some kind of lackey. Damn that general.*

Sarcastic and petulant, Oleg leaned into the driver's window to scold his subordinates. "You two went globe-trotting without my knowledge or permission. There is such a thing as chain of command, and you ambitious up-and-comers violated the code. You kept your boss in the dark."

"Oleg," Tanya said from the passenger seat, "like you, we're soldiers in the service of the *Rodina*. We take orders from the general. If you have a problem, take it up with him."

Taken aback at the tone of Tanya's voice, Oleg asked, "Where are we going?"

"To the north shore of Long Island," Grigori answered. "We have something to show you at the Russian UN ambassador's residence. Hop in."

As Oleg settled into the backseat, Tanya and Grigori exchanged glances. An unspoken message passed between them. *Now we know where your car is parked. Das Sveedaneeya, Oleg.*

Grigori used the extensive parkway and expressway system of Long Island to get to the ambassador's residence at Killenworth Estate in Glen Cove. Security cameras zoomed onto the Range Rover. Satisfied the occupants were legitimate visitors, two steel gates opened automatically. The Rover parked behind a carriage house, now home to a jihad terrorist.

"What's the story behind this mansion?" Oleg asked.

Grigori answered, "Killenworth Estate is owned by the Russian government. It has been the home of the Russian ambassador to the United Nations since World War II. The mansion is smack in the middle of Long Island's famous Gold Coast, but off the beaten path. During the cold war, Nikita Khrushchev and Fidel Castro used Killenworth separately."

"How's the security?" Oleg said.

"As you saw when we drove in, Killenworth is surrounded by a ten-foot-high concrete wall, topped with coils of barbed wire. One electronically controlled metal double gate allows for entry and exit. The gate is covered twenty-four seven by handpicked *Spetsnaz* security. Always two men on, two off, and two in reserve. No one enters or leaves the Carriage House without their approval. O'Leary's only visitor is Tanya, and he thrives on her company. *Spetsnaz* use infrared pan, tilt, and zoom cameras around the clock."

"I don't see many cars parked in the lot," Oleg said.

"That's because the UN ambassador no longer uses it as a primary residence. He and his staff come here for an occasional weekend soiree, but it's empty most of the time. The ambassador and his crew have apartments in New York City. Our countrymen love the fleshpots of Manhattan. Our countrywomen love to go shopping. Our people are born partiers. There's ample time to rest in our graves. We're careful when we come and go. The FBI has surveillance cameras and listening devices mounted outside the gate. We transported our assassin in the rear of a delivery van. No one but no one knows he's in the basement," Grigori concluded.

"Come and meet Andrew O'Leary," Tanya said.

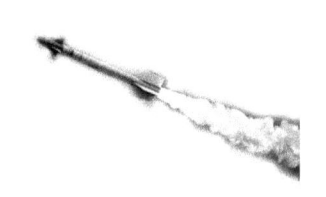

CHAPTER EIGHTEEN

Isis Terrorist

Oleg, Grigori, and Tanya went down concrete steps into a musty basement.

"I'm uncomfortable in the presence of others at prayer," Oleg said as he gazed at shoeless O'Leary, on his knees facing east toward Mecca, praying to Allah.

Peering at O'Leary through a one-way mirror, Oleg smelled the scent of Tanya's perfume. His eyes locked on to her legs and buttocks. Grigori stood off to the side. Oleg was indifferent to his aftershave odor.

"So, Tanya Veronika," Oleg said, "tell me all about this little shit secret agent from ISIS."

"Grigori and I learned he was searching for a sympathetic imam to inspire him to jihad. Floundering around, O'Leary wanted to visit Syria and train as a jihadist warrior. He needed some direction, and we provided it. A graduate of Long Island University with a degree in computer science, he hooked up with some 'radicals' who pretended to be students. In reality, they were on our payroll. First order of business was to bar O'Leary from using the Internet, cell phone, and house phone. The FBI calls it 'writing on the wall.' It's common knowledge the FBI uses undercover spies to set up kids. O'Leary assumed our people weren't FBI undercover agents since they discouraged the use of computers. We made him anonymous, flying under the radar. Our radicals supplied him with a ticket to Istanbul where we 'accidentally' stumbled upon O'Leary at the giant Hagia Sophia mosque. O'Leary's family believes he's vagabonding through Europe."

"He practices Islam?"

"*Da*, Oleg Arturovich. You saw the yellow arrow painted on his wall?"

"*Da*."

"We painted it to point east, in the direction of Mecca, Saudi Arabia. Five times a day, O'Leary drops to his knees on a *seggadah*, a prayer mat, supplied by us. Following the direction of the arrow, he prays to Allah for the honor of a martyr's death. Occasionally, I see tears rolling down his chin. He's perfect for the mission."

"Maybe perfect for now, but for how long? You expect to keep him cooped up in a room like a gulag solitary confinement cell. I see no television, no radio, no computer, no books, and no magazines other than the Koran on his bed. What else keeps him from going stir-crazy?"

"Me. Every other night I come to his bed and promise him an eternity of sex. He says I will go to the front of the line ahead of his seventy-two virgin wives. Everyone else will wait their turn. He's convinced we're going to pony ride the missile into the aircraft."

"Tell me more, Tanya Veronika."

"Well, we used our contacts and thousands of dollars to smuggle O'Leary into Syria. Our people hooked him up with an ISIS Syrian unit where he went through three months of terrorist boot camp. Long Island college boy learned how to fire automatic rifles, pistols, machine guns, throw hand grenades, and construct IED explosives. He was also instructed in suicide tactics because he checked a box on an ISIS application."

"Application? What do you mean?" Oleg said.

"ISIS is no different from any other army," Tanya said. "They want to check out the skill levels of applicants and ask them pages of questions. One of those questions is if you prefer to be a fighter or a martyr. O'Leary checked the box marked martyr. He was accepted and went into three months of rigorous training. After graduation, O'Leary put his name on the map with ISIS. He pulled off a big caper in Syria."

"How so?"

"Grigori and I fed him information about an arsenal of Grinch missiles at Tabqa air base in Raqqa Province. O'Leary and a handpicked crew made off with a truckload of launchers and missiles. The ISIS bandits used a convoy of stolen American trucks to carry away the loot. ISIS intends to use the Grinches on American military aircraft, sticking their thumb in the Americans' eye. News of the missile theft has been leaked to the media. Al Jazeera printed it, then the story went viral. When American planes fall to the ground, ISIS will proudly take the credit and the blame."

"Tell me," Oleg said, "how do we know your little ISIS shit knows how to use the Grinch?"

"Good question. O'Leary went through extensive Grinch training. He's an expert on loading the launcher, targeting a plane, aiming, trajectory, and timing. His training included taking out drones. He's ready to do the job."

"How much does he know about the job?"

"Just enough. We've made no mention of Long Beach. He believes Allah has selected him for a mission, whatever it is. He doesn't want to know and doesn't care. Paradise, yours truly, and my seventy-two virgin sisters-in-law are all our boy needs."

Oleg nodded approval. "You two have done well, but we must continue to remain dark. No communications on your phones and computers, unless absolutely necessary. The FBI agents are like bloodhounds sniffing all over the Internet. There's too much at stake for a slipup. Total lockdown until we finalize the purchase of the Aqua units.

"You've hung an ISIS black flag on the wall. What does the lettering say?"

"The text follows fundamental Muslim belief. It reads, 'No God but Allah' and 'Mohammad is the messenger of God'," Tanya said. "I drape it over the one-way mirror so dirty old men don't come around at night like peeping toms."

Oleg smiled at the veiled insult. "Come, let's have some lunch where we may sit down and talk."

"Before lunch, we want to take you to a black site for a look at the Grinch," Tanya said.

As they went for the door, Oleg motioned to a pair of waiting *Spetsnaz* security men. Pointing to O'Leary's room, he said, "He's yours for now. No mistakes, men."

"*Da, tovarich*," they said and saluted.

CHAPTER NINETEEN

ARSENAL

Grigori's olive green Range Rover passed through the security gate, leaving Killenworth in the rearview mirror.

"The FBI will run a license plate check. It will come back to a dead letter box in the Bronx," Grigori said. "Our images will be hard to verify. The windows are over-tinted, a violation of the New York State traffic laws."

Three Russian barracudas made their way south along Glen Cove Road. Turning east onto Old Country Road, they journeyed to a seedy factory-residential district in Westbury. Sitting at the dead end of Coventry Lane was a decrepit auto-repair shop. A weather-beaten sign with faded and missing letters hung over the entrance to the single-story building. Three-foot-high red letters read "--TO R—AIR." Emphasizing the dinginess, boarded-up windows and two junk autos were parked in the lot, one without tires. A locked chain-link fence warded off intruders.

"I'll never get used to the dreariness of this place," Grigori said. "Barrels of motor oil have seeped into the ground over the years. Oil may leech into the water table and become a health hazard."

"Possibly. We won't be around here long enough to watch the American EPA dig up the grounds," Tanya said as Grigori unlocked the gate.

Pressing a remote-control button which he removed from the glove compartment, Grigori raised the automatic garage door. He maneuvered his Rover into the bay, with nothing but overhead fluorescent lights and two more junk autos that had never felt the swipe of a dustcloth. The place reeked of mold, oil, grease, urine, and lack of fresh air.

Leaving the Rover, Grigori went to a far wall, flicked a light switch, and opened the electric power box. He punched a code into a keypad and slid a wall, like a shower door panel, to reveal a secret room. Three Russians stepped into a large walk-in vault the size of a one-car garage.

Two picnic tables filled the room. Each was laid out with two padlocked green metal containers resembling closed coffins.

"I take it each case is holding a Grinch and heat-seeking missile," Oleg said.

"*Da*, the smaller, thinner tube is the missile," Tanya said. "Each apparatus is primed and ready for launch."

"Why two Grinches?"

"Oleg Arturovich, plans change. We have a contingency plan in case Moscow orders more than one strike," Grigori said.

Oleg sucked in a breath. He grasped Grigori's meaning of "Moscow orders." *My subordinates are clearly working outside of the chain of command leaving me blind, dumb, and out of the loop. Russian Revenge sucks*, he thought.

CHAPTER TWENTY

BLINDSIDED

"General Stankovich neglected to fill me in. I know nothing about a second mission."

Trying to maintain his composure, Oleg said, "I see two sealed garment bags. What's in them?"

Tanya strode to the black plastic bags and unzipped the one closest to her. Shucking the bag cover revealed a multi-pocketed vest. Oleg's eyes darted from the vest to a pair of locked green wood boxes lying on the floor.

"Are they suicide vests? Why the hell do we need suicide vests? Who—and what—is to be blown up? By what authority did you two introduce suicide vests to the project?"

Grigori took the lead. "Oleg Arturovich, the reason we avoided lunch and came to this place was on the general's orders. He knew you would have questions. Our instructions have come from the highest authority. It was felt you should be spoon-fed the details. This is a multiple-strike mission. New orders have been passed down to destroy two planes and unleash Muslim suicide bombers on crowded venues. ISIS loves to pull off spectacular events. Our bosses are convinced President Obama will be outraged to the point of demanding that Congress formally declare war on ISIS and its allies. When war is declared, generals and admirals will take command and ravage the lands occupied by ISIS, Al-Qaeda,

Al-Shabab, Boko Haram, and every other terrorist army. The slaughter will make Hitler's invasion of the Soviet Union look like boys playing in a sandbox."

"So, Grigori Viktorovich, who is working for whom? Am I being recalled to Moscow for, as they used to say, severe punishment?"

"*Nyet, tovarich*, as long as you support Operation Russian Revenge," Grigori said. His cold hard eyes reinforced the message. Oleg imagined Grigori morphing into a swaying cobra about to sink his fangs into an unsuspecting victim.

"Fair enough. Tell me the truth about the scope of the project, and I'll respond with a truthful answer."

Tanya piped up, "O'Leary is one of two men recruited to be missile launchers. Like O'Leary, the other is also a radicalized American student hellbent on making Allah proud. Assassin number two has been trained to target an incoming plane at LaGuardia Airport. The airport depends on a landing strip alongside the Grand Central Parkway leaving planes only three hundred or so feet above the moving cars, the height of a football field. He hasn't been told about the target. We can't miss."

"How do suicide bombers fit into this mosaic?"

Tanya continued, "We have recruited two attractive women to wear the vests. They're Muslims and wear Western attire. Unlike their male counterparts, they aren't students. Born in Pakistan, they come to the U.S. with hate. To them, all Americans are godless infidels and blasphemers, deserving of death. Targets haven't been finalized, but we penciled in Penn Station and one to be determined."

"Young warriors, this morning, I complimented the general upon the simplicity of the plan. 'Very few moving parts' was the expression I used. Now, I learn we have multiple targets, many moving parts and assassins. The chances for a blunder have increased. This thing can backfire on the *Rodina*. It's complicated, like trying to do brain surgery, a heart transplant, and an appendectomy at the same time. The risks for failure are astronomical. I don't think I can go along with the program. It looks like a blueprint for disaster, and I have been doing this stuff for all of my adult life."

"Oleg Arturovich," Tanya said, "we follow orders. Grigori has put it to you. Are you with us or against us, *tovarich*?" Tanya walked away, leaving Oleg with a clear view of her buttocks.

Oleg, sensing he might wind up in the trunk of a junk auto, decided to bide his time. Lust-filled eyes followed Tanya as she walked off. "You have my assurance of complete cooperation. I will arrange for all the dollars you need to fulfill your mission. Does that satisfy both of you?"

The last words Oleg heard in this life came from Grigori. "*Das Sveedaneeya*," he said, as a bullet from a .40 caliber Glock penetrated Oleg's skull, spiraling his Panama hat across the room. The dead man's face crashed onto the filthy concrete floor. Grigori straddled the corpse, pocketed Oleg's Ray-Ban sunglasses, and fired a second round into the dead man's skull. Blood seeped from the head wounds and tried to blend in with the oil-stained floor. Instead, it settled on top of the grime. "Nothing doing. Blood is blood and oil is oil. Some things don't mix," Grigori said.

Tanya and Grigori breathed in the smell of gunpowder as they held hands over the dead body of their late comrade. "Moving parts. We should etch those words onto Oleg's headstone," Tanya said.

"Tanya Veronika, what headstone?"

Grigori returned to his Rover, retrieved a shovel, and slipped out of the back door. He returned fifteen minutes later, carrying his suit coat and shovel, head covered with beads of sweat.

Dragging Oleg's remains to a shallow grave behind the shop, Grigori used his right foot to shove the body into the ground. He thought about snatching Oleg's Rolex, but thought, *not a good idea. General Stankovich would consider me a grave robber. Not a good career move.*

Rolling Oleg's body into the pit, Grigori tossed the Panama hat and Ray-Bans on the corpse and pulled a set of car keys from Oleg's pocket. Shoveling dirt on the body, Grigori said, "This is for the *Rodina*. Nothing else matters."

BOOK THREE

The Chinese used gunpowder to make fireworks for celebrations. The white man came along and said, 'Holy shit, we can use this to kill people. What a better way to celebrate than that?'

Jarod Kintz
Seriously Delirious

CHAPTER TWENTY-ONE

Board Meeting

Jules Goldberg, owner of unit 705, called a board meeting on Monday morning, April 18. With him were Marvin Taub, Isidore Diamond, owner of penthouse 806, and Stu Rabinowitz. Jules carried one proxy vote in his pocket, belonging to Anthony Palumbo, in case of a tie. Desperate to unload his unit for a big profit, Jules carried the proxy like a crooked poker player hiding an ace up his sleeve.

Questions came flying. "What's the Russian guy's name? Is he a diplomat? Why all the interest in the Aqua and Long Beach? Is he an arms dealer? Why send his son on a deal of this magnitude? What's with all the security enhancements?"

Stuart Rabinowitz, owner of a second-floor unit, said, "I'm not selling my place. I love Long Beach, but I don't want to live in a citadel surrounded by armed guards wearing Ninja outfits. Long Beach isn't South Africa following the election of Nelson Mandela when white homeowners lived in fear, surrounding their homes and farmsteads with armed militia. You guys will leave here with wheelbarrows of cash. There's nothing in it for me. Let the Russians whore around with the oil sheikhs on the French Riviera. This sounds like a bunch of drug dealers setting up a cocaine warehouse. Can't you guys see them shuttling their cargo from a fleet of ships lying offshore? How about the sight of narcotics cops rappelling down the side of the condo. This thing stinks."

Goldberg's business judgment had taken root in his backside. Motivated by a quick profit and a hundred-thousand-dollar bribe from the general, he tried to mollify Rabinowitz.

"Stu, take it easy. We'll check out the broker and buyer. I have a relationship with the owner of the real-estate agency, Cookie Weinstein. Cookie's been in the business since Nixon was president. She's straight and wouldn't stick her neck out for drug merchants. Cookie lost her youngest son to a heroin overdose—dead at twenty-one. Never got over it, as you would expect."

"All right, Jules. Maybe drug dealers is a stretch, but I've been around long enough to smell a shit sandwich regardless of how much mustard is smeared on the bread."

"Stu, be patient," Jules said. "I'll put your concerns in a memo and send it to every apartment owner."

Still uncertain, Rabinowitz folded his arms. "I'll wait for the memo and feedback from my fellow future victims," he said with dripping sarcasm.

Goldberg rolled his eyes. "Stu, this is a good deal. Your monthly maintenance charges and taxes will be reduced to nothing. Think of all the time and money you can spend in Resorts World Casino at Aqueduct Racetrack."

Rabinowitz rose and shouted, "How the hell do you know about my private life, Jules?"

Jules went right back at his opponent and said, "I know lots of things. How do you think I keep my position on the board? I'll update you after I speak to Cookie. Meeting's over."

"No, it's not," Rabinowitz said. "I have questions."

Jules, who regarded Stu as a pain in the ass stood over him and took control. "Well, let's delve into the questions asked at the top of the meeting. Russian daddy's name is Artur Glinka, and he's no diplomat. Since the rise of Putin, Mr. Glinka has salted away billions in oil profits. He owns half of the oil in the Caucasus Mountains, including the Baku oil fields. Buying a few condo units amounts to chump change for

Glinka. Donald Trump's money looks like pocket change compared with Glinka's."

"Why Long Beach, Jules? After all, it's a nice place, but our beach isn't the pearl of the Atlantic Ocean," Stu said.

"Good question. Glinka and some of his cronies are degenerate gamblers. The reason for the helicopter is to provide a quick zip to Atlantic City or Mohegan Sun. These guys can make or drop millions of dollars in a night and think nothing of it. For some reason, Daddy gets a big kick out of impressing prostitutes—who, I might add, seem to hang onto him for dear life."

"Oil is one thing," Stu said, "drugs are a more sinister issue. What about weapons of war? Is Glinka an arms dealer on the side?"

"Nothing but oil on his resume, Stu, I don't think he needs to sell either drugs or arms to make money," Jules said.

"Why, Jules? There's a lot of money in those products."

"Come over to the window. Take a hard look at a sight you see every day, a chain of cargo ships and tankers at anchor. The big fat mamas are tankers, and each one is carrying over one hundred thousand barrels of refined oil. When they finally dock at Port Newark, just one tanker unloads enough fuel to supply every gas station from the Battery Tunnel to Montauk Point for a month. There's more money in 'black gold' than in drugs and arms. Besides, oil is legal. Put your fears to bed, Stu."

"OK, OK, Jules," Izzy Diamond said. "You're a good salesman. I'll give you that. Tell us more about the Bolsheviks."

CHAPTER TWENTY-TWO

SMELLING A RAT

Jules waited for the question. He pulled an ace from his sleeve. "Are you familiar with Hyde Park in London, Izzy?"

Diamond, a man who had accumulated wealth in the jewelry business, squinted and thought of his answer. "By reputation only, Jules. Hyde Park is a ritzy neighborhood for the English lords and ladies to lounge around London town."

"Correct, Izzy. My friend Cookie, through her real-estate contacts, came up with a building in London that is a clone of what our Russian buyers want to create at the Aqua."

Izzy Diamond was knuckling under. The lure of a quick sale with an incredible profit built in clouded his business sense. "Go ahead, Jules. What's with London?"

"The building is high-end residential with many wealthy international owners. It's an elegant fortress with bulletproof glass, a secure elevator, armed guards, and innumerable closed-circuit TV cameras. It's known as a 'secure building.' According to Cookie, Hyde Park is dotted with secure buildings, off limits to all but the very rich."

Digesting Cookie's information, the board leaned toward taking on the idea. The vision of financial rewards began to outweigh the negatives.

Stuart Rabinowitz raised his hand. Dressed in a white terry-cloth robe with flip-flop sandals, Rabinowitz had just been to the Aqua's gym and swimming pool. Stuart's perfect hair and pearly teeth matched the terry-cloth robe.

"What's on your mind, Stu?" Jules said.

Stu placed his hand under his chin and said, "Early on in this debate, someone mentioned the Russian broker and buyer grew up in Grozny. My ancestors came from Grozny, thrown out during one of the czar's pogroms. Not for nothing, but there are more mosques in Grozny than churches. Chechnya is next door to Dagestan, where the Boston Marathon pressure-cooker bombers were spawned. Grozny is the capital of Chechnya. Muslim rebels have been at war with Moscow since 1990. They're the madmen who took over a movie theater in Moscow and held an entire grade school hostage. Many people died in those terrorist attacks. Are we opening the floodgates for Muslims? I don't want those people in my house. I don't like them. I don't like their religion, and until I'm satisfied the broker and buyer aren't Muslims, I'll fight all of you on this sale."

Goldberg, Taub, and Diamond were speechless. Neither man had given this angle a bit of thought. The matter had devolved into unforeseen territory. Jules retreated to his salesman experience. He felt it would be unwise to spring the proxy votes on the owners at this time. He thought of a way out, for now.

"Stu, you raised an important point," Jules finally said. "I happen to know Glinka is not a Muslim surname. As for the agent, we'll check her out. This isn't something the board can decide, in spite of the fact that we could technically approve the deal. We'll conduct due diligence on your points and make an intelligent presentation to all the residents. We'll meet again next Friday, April twenty-second, at ten a.m."

CHAPTER TWENTY-THREE

MOVING TO THE FRONT LINES

Austin Boulevard in Oceanside sits north of Long Beach City. General Stankovich had set up a breakfast meeting at a luncheonette in a strip mall, diminishing a chance encounter with Aqua owners.

Arriving by Trek bicycle, as usual, Stankovich passed himself off as an aging beach bum, the kind of man one neither notices nor remembers. Dressed in his standard grungy sneakers, an armpit-stained T-shirt and cutoff jeans, he further disguised himself with a crash helmet and sunglasses. After chaining his bike to a metal rack, the general removed his helmet, donned a Mets baseball cap, and waited for his crew.

Tanya and Grigori parked their Range Rover at the far end of the mall and ambled over to the entrance. Stankovich had issued a strong suggestion to dress down and keep a low profile. No high heels for Tanya, her hair was in a bun, and she wore no makeup. Grigori, as was his custom, trailed behind in a T-shirt and cutoff denim jeans with flip-flops.

Russian to the core, Tanya and Grigori waited for a nod from the general as to where to sit. Deferring to his wish, they took a corner booth. A portly middle-aged waitress served coffee and tea for the general. Her upper left arm bore a reading, "Property of Jason," with chains surrounding the message.

"I've never developed a taste for coffee," the general said. "*Chai* or tea is my drink of choice, that is, when good Russian vodka is not available."

His subordinates smiled. Stankovich's love of vodka was legendary. It was claimed by people at a Moscow reception that they watched the general polish off two liters of straight vodka. He went about his business without a stagger or slur.

"You're a vodka man, General?" Grigori said, knowing the answer.

"*Da*, but not today. Business now, drink later," Stankovich said. "How are we doing with the ISIS wannabes? Are they still up for martyrdom? Are they in safekeeping?"

"I'll begin with O'Leary," Tanya said. "He's still at Killenworth studying the Koran, praying five times a day, and dreaming about me. He's like a cloistered monk and quite at peace. No worries with that fellow."

"And the other man, Tanya. Is he under control?"

"*Da*, General. George Hoffman has volunteered for a mission. He wants to launch his Grinch today and has invented a war name: Yusuf Al-Muslim. He hasn't been told either the details or the location. Our only problem is holding him back."

"Tell me again, where did you find this Hoffman?"

"He was recruited at the same time as O'Leary, drifting around, looking for action and recognition. They didn't know each other until we landed them in Syria for terrorist training camp. They met in the ISIS barracks and became friends. We knew it would happen."

"How so?" asked the general.

"They come from the same neighborhood, went to similar schools and university. Well educated, spoke the same language, and were raised in religious homes. Hoffman is Roman Catholic. Despite their different religions, it was natural to bond with each other. Hoffman is a graduate of the state university at Stony Brook with an engineering degree. He owns a bright intellect, but lacks maturity. I call him my man-child."

"Explain, Tanya. What is this man-child?"

"That's my term for a person with the body of a man equipped with the mind of a child. Chaps like Hoffman and O'Leary are classic case studies of arrested development. Psychologists claim they are searching for certainty under a more fancy term, cognitive closure. Spoiled brats who have had every door opened for them—they are nothing but large children. They can't seem to get past today. Instant gratification and rewards are like heroin to them. One reason for their addiction to video games is they usually win. Our assassins are from the little-league-baseball generation where every child on the team gets a trophy. No achievement is necessary, except to show up and park your ass on the dugout bench. If we didn't find them, they would have found us."

"Where is Hoffman's bed? Is it secure?"

"The Catskill Mountains are his secluded hideaway. He's in a small A-frame ski and hunting lodge in Roscoe, New York, the southern end of the mountain range. It takes two and a half hours of driving, and the place has a private road, surrounded by New York State lands. It's perfect. Ski and hunting seasons are over. Summer vacations are two months away. It's quiet, and our security force is competent, equal to the task."

General Stankovich pondered his next question. It had overt sexual overtones. "Tanya, are you friendly with this Hoffman? You know what I mean by friendly?"

"*Da*, General, not to the extent of O'Leary's sexual dependence. Since Hoffman is in the mountains, my visits are sporadic. I did manage to have him pose for a martyrdom video cradling a Grinch in his arms. For that achievement, I am friendly with the man."

Stankovich smiled inwardly, thinking, *If I were younger, Tanya, I'd give you a run for your money.*

"Property of Jason" waitress returned for breakfast orders of omelets and toast with coffee and tea refills. Stankovich watched as she walked off. "I wonder if she has chains tattooed around that big ass. Imagine, the creature proudly advertises she belongs to a man. Perhaps the lady never heard of the American Emancipation Proclamation. Now, someone fill me in on the status of the women."

"That's my department," Grigori said. "My girls are more rabid than Hoffman and O'Leary put together. Those chaps have grown full black beards. I shared their photos with Qahira and Malak to give them the impression the men are potential future husbands in Paradise. The women are Muslim partisans, dedicated to the cause. Prayers for martyrdom dominate their form of liturgy. Five times a day, each of them faces east on their knees and vows jihad. I am told they have saved their virginity for the first night in Paradise."

"Where are they, Grigori?"

"In the same safe house in Roscoe waiting for their orders. The girls are as anxious as I am, General."

"Be patient. Eat your breakfast, then we talk. Thank you for disposing of Oleg. He had the potential of folding up and turning us in to the FBI. Silence for now, the slave lady is bringing plates."

As directed, they ate without conversation waiting for a cue from the general.

CHAPTER TWENTY-FOUR
OPERATIONS ORDERS

"I have selected the day or, more accurately, the night for the operations. All actions will take place on Friday evening, July eighth," Stankovich said.

Tanya and Grigori pushed away their plates and leaned across to face the general.

"Friday night in July, General? May I know what led to that decision?" Tanya asked.

"*Da*, Tanya. The Americans like to celebrate their rebellion with fireworks spectacles. They call them pyrotechnic displays. On the fourth of July, they put on a big show at Jones Beach for the Long Island residents. Likewise, Macy's department store puts on an extravaganza for the Manhattan and New Jersey crowd on the East and Hudson rivers. Long Beach can't compete against those lavish overkills. The city managers opted to have their fireworks on the Friday following the fourth of July. This year it falls on July eighth."

"Why at night, General?" Grigori said.

"Because, my young friends, the sun doesn't set until nine p.m. in July, which is the time the fireworks are set off. At the same time, Europe-bound jumbo jets, packed with vacationing tourists, go wheels up out of JFK Airport. Our Grinch launcher will have a pick of targets. By six p.m., the local police shut down access to the beach and boardwalk.

From that time on, the place is bursting with spectators. At fireworks time, most of the crowd is drunk. The city is in a frenzy putting up comfort stations along the street side of the boardwalk. Most drunks don't bother to stand on line. They piss over the boardwalk guardrail. Mardi Gras in New Orleans meets Long Beach. It's all the cops can do to keep order, and people like us up on a penthouse courtyard roof aren't even noticed."

"Where do the fireworks come from, General? Do they launch them from the jetties?" Tanya said.

Stankovich folded his arms, in the manner of Italian dictator Benito Mussolini. He set his jaw and orated a speech he had apparently practiced.

"A barge is anchored one hundred yards to the sea from the Lincoln Boulevard jetty. Computers are preprogrammed to ignite the rockets. Simultaneously, O'Leary will launch his Grinch into the sky and take down an airplane. Before the drunks realize the burning plane isn't part of the show, you will dispose of O'Leary with a gunshot to his temple. I will take the pistol you used on Oleg and replace it with an untraceable Glock. I don't want FBI ballistics experts comparing bullets from Oleg's head to those in O'Leary's brain. Leave the gun near the body. Don't forget to place the ISIS flag in his vicinity. Make it look like a suicide. We'll release his suicide/martyrdom video and America will be off to wage World War III on ISIS. The warmongers have the statistics to back them up. My research has shown to date that ISIS is directly responsible for seventy terrorist attacks around the world, from Indonesia to Paris. The Middle East won't have anything left but oil, mangy flea-infested camels and bedouins. Then we move in and pump the oil for a thirsty world. OPEC be damned. We'll charge top dollar or euro. The USSR will fly the Hammer and Sickle once again."

Tanya was amazed at the rigid tone of the general's voice. She thought to tone him down and distract his thinking.

"Does one downed plane actually lead to all that, General?"

"*Nyet*. Not in itself. Your Hoffman lover will be transported in a customized truck to a service road near LaGuardia Airport, where he will stick his Grinch missile into the belly of an inbound domestic jumbo jet. After the trigger is pulled, the ISIS wannabe will suffer the same fate as O'Leary. Hoffman will have his ticket punched and join O'Leary on the paradise express. His video will go viral with the help of Al Jazeera. I saw the video and must say, the chap put on an Oscar-winning performance. 'You will suffer to the gates of hell and burn for all eternity,' he boasted, meaning his own countrymen. The videos are what American prosecutors like to call 'the smoking gun'."

"What's in store for the women, the suicide bombers?" Tanya said.

"Tell her, Grigori. It's all right. We're near the end," Stankovich said.

Grigori turned in his booth seat to face Tanya. "They refer to themselves as *shahida,* female martyrs. Each has a pseudonym. Qahira translates to victorious and Malak means angel in Urdu or Pakistani. Qahira's target is the baseball park Citi Field in Queens. The Mets are playing a night game against their rivals, the Washington Nationals. Game time is seven ten p.m. Qahira will soon start as a seasonal hostess to service the box-seat owners around the visitor's dugout. Security is lax for employees, especially beautiful young women. Qahira plans to smuggle in pounds of explosives piecemeal. They're stuffed with ball bearings and will be stored in her locker. No one in the Nationals' dugout or surrounding seats will survive. I do believe the game will have to be called since the Nationals will be turned into globs of bleeding flesh. Qahira will do her job while the Mets are on the field, guaranteeing maximum damage to the visitors."

"Grigori, why destroy the Nationals? The Mets are a beloved home team, always regarded as the underdog. Americans love the underdog. Surely, the destruction of a New York baseball team would gain worldwide attention," Tanya said.

"The Nationals home field is in Washington, DC, at the Robert F. Kennedy Memorial Stadium. Their elimination, although symbolic, represents the American Eagle. Qahira has paid attention to this detail in her martyrdom video. 'Death to the Washington infidels,' she proclaimed."

"Besides, the general is a Mets fan," Grigori said, pointing out the orange-and-blue logo on Stankovich's baseball cap.

Stankovich sipped on his tea, smiled, and nodded for Grigori to continue.

"Malak the Angel has been given the piece-de-resistance, the icing on the cake. Since eighth of July is Friday, the Jewish Sabbath begins at sundown. We have assigned her to a synagogue in lower Manhattan with a congregation of about a hundred people. Surveillance has shown they tend to show up regularly and on time, winter or summer. The place has been selected because it's out of the way, has no security, and is the earliest house of worship erected by the Jews when they arrived in New York City. Malak's video begins and ends with the chant, 'Death to Israel. Allahu Akbar'. She can't wait to do the deed."

Stankovich slid his teacup across the table, waved off "Property of Jason," and leaned into the faces of his young subordinates.

"Timing is critical. Citi-Field and the synagogue are manageable. The set bomb time nine p.m. The planes are somewhat more tricky. LaGuardia is a lesser problem than JFK. Due to the Mets baseball game, it's customary to divert incoming planes from the stadium to the target area because noise from descending aircraft can disturb the pitcher's concentration. Complaints were registered, probably some money changed hands, and planes are now directed onto a landing strip off the Grand Central Parkway. They come roaring in like marching bands in a parade, one after the other. We have timed them as having a three-minute separation—nine p.m. is doable. That makes for three simultaneous bombings."

"What about number four, the big one at Long Beach, General?" Tanya said.

"The schedule lists a smorgasbord of targets. Like the repeated landings at LaGuardia, the JFK planes take off in rapid succession. Many of them are bound for European destinations with stopovers in London, Paris, and beyond. I've selected three with a departure near the eight thirty p. m. mark. Delays are inevitable, especially on a Friday night in July. At nightfall, our target will come out of its hangar to meet the Grinch. I'm allowing for a window of between nine and nine fifteen p. m. By then, the other events will have gone down and the broadcasts will be all over the police radios and news media, causing confusion and panic inside New York City. The Americans have an old saying—fast food is junk food and fast news is junk news. They're correct. The story will make the rounds and be a diversion during the initial stages. By nine thirty, a JFK plane will be a pile of smoldering debris in the Long Beach ocean. The whole thing will be over. We leave the country. I have a helicopter on standby at the rebuilt Long Beach Hospital emergency room. The good city managers had the foresight to include a heliport on the grounds."

"Where are we bound for, General?"

"On my orders, on the morning of the eighth, one of the cargo ships lying offshore will weigh anchor and head out to the open sea. That won't attract attention. The only regulation is our captain must notify the Coast Guard within a reasonable time. No one will pay attention as ships leave to make for another port where their cargo may be unloaded for a more lucrative profit than in either New York or New Jersey. Our ship is equipped with a helipad, and we'll be long gone before the sun rises on Saturday morning. Are there any questions?"

Grigori and Tanya sat silent, digesting the implications of the breakfast meeting. No one asked a question.

"All right, then. You have your assignments. Grigori, a man is waiting near your car. He will hand over two suitcases, each containing five million dollars in one-hundred-dollar bills. Use the money to purchase the Grinch's launching platform. Don't worry about setbacks. We have an insider. A board member is on our payroll."

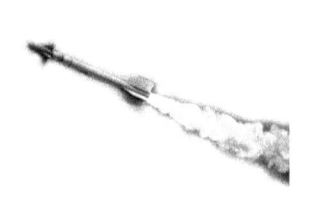

CHAPTER TWENTY-FIVE
CLOSING THE DEAL

Jules Goldberg and Marvin Taub waited in Taub's penthouse unit. Grigori, Tanya, Rabinowitz, and Diamond had not yet arrived. *This deal has to go through or I'm out of money, and maybe a thumb or two*, Taub thought.

It had been a long week for each man, motivated by his unique needs. Regardless of personal trepidations, the sellers were anxious to seal the deal. Each sat quietly, dwelling on the mother lode of profits about to be received.

Taub, who had millions of dollars on the brain, was speculating on his new life free of an ex-wife, alimony payments, and loan sharks. He thought, *I've been down this road many times. Money is like an eel in the hand. It could wriggle away as fast as one latched onto it.*

Taub said to Goldberg, "Where the hell are the Russkies? We set the meeting for two o'clock. Izzy and Stu haven't shown their faces."

Jules glanced at this watch. "Ten minutes to go, Marvin. Don't look hungry. They may offer less if they see sweat pouring from your forehead."

"I don't sweat, Jules. You think I just fell off the back of a turnip truck. I've spent a lifetime cutting deals. They want what I've got. If the money is right, they can have the unit. This has to be a cash deal.

If my ex finds out about the sale, she'll steal me blind. If no cash, they get nothing because I'll wind up with nothing."

Jules cut in. "Marvin, I feel the same way. I want to meet Mr. Green. I'm not taking a check from some Russian bank or other off-the-wall place. Besides, Mr. Green allows us to avoid capital-gains taxes."

"You're right, Jules. Capital gains is a curse for people like us. We work all our lives, take risks, stay up nights worrying, build up a little nest egg, and have it stolen by the government. If the crooks spent it on worthwhile programs, I might not mind as much. Instead, they piss it away on 'entitlements' for a bunch of losers. I'm with you on meeting Mr. Green. Dollars in my pocket feels good."

A phone call to Taub from concierge security interrupted the talk of money.

"Mr. Diamond and Mr. Rabinowitz are on the way up. Is that OK?"

"Sure, let them in the elevator. I've been expecting them," a relieved Taub told the guard.

As the four men gathered around Taub's couch, they engaged in small talk.

"Nice day, Marvin," Diamond said.

Rabinowitz shrugged. "It's always nice in Long Beach, Izzy. That's why we live here. I'm pleased the Russians will see another fine view from the penthouse courtyard. It should help with the sale. In real-estate terms, instead of curb appeal, we have beach appeal."

Marvin picked up the ringing phone. "Send her up," he repeated to the guard, raising his right thumb.

Tanya strode through the foyer wheeling two black suitcases behind her. All the men ogled the cases, forgetting about Tanya for the moment. Taub offered cocktails, expecting a negative answer.

"No, thank you, Mr. Taub. Never while I work. It tends to cloud the judgment," Tanya said.

"I agree, Tanya. You've brought something with you to the meeting," Taub said, pointing to the suitcases.

"Yes. Before we get into the contents, my client wants to settle on selling prices. I ran the sales comparisons for the area before the meeting. I know what was paid for unit 806 last year. I am also well informed as to the purchase prices for units 705 and 805. My client is willing to compensate each of you at a reasonable profit for the units."

Goldberg, about to say something, was quieted by Taub.

"I've got this, Jules. Penthouse 806 is for sale at what you call a reasonable profit. However, I have come to love the place, the view, and the company of the other owners. We're like family, and I don't want to sell unless there is a compelling reason."

"Fair enough, Mr. Taub. What's your compelling reason?" Tanya said.

"The number I mentioned last week to you and Grigori has gone up. I want four million dollars, and that's not negotiable. I won't haggle with you. That's my drop-dead offer. Take it or leave it, Tanya."

Taub did not regret his offer. A weekly poker player, Taub read his opponent's body language. *I'm going to get the four million dollars,* he thought, *and it's sitting in one of those suitcases with a lot of relatives. Damn.*

Tanya Dubov, a daughter of Mother Russia, also knew a thing or two about body language. She noticed Taub's eyes never left the suitcases. She knew he was sending an unconscious signal he needed the money. She also knew mob guys were looking for him. The kind of men who either break your legs or cut off a thumb to send a message. Loan sharks didn't get their name and reputation by accident.

Taub rubbed his knees and looked at his right thumb. He was about to break into a sweat. "Tanya, show me what's in your satchels. Make my day."

Tanya raised four fingers and said, "Before I show you anything, I want to finalize the numbers. Mr. Diamond, are you agreeable to the same amount for the penthouse unit at four million dollars?"

Diamond knew if he balked, Tanya would pick up the cases and go down the elevator as fast as she had come up. He nodded his head and said, "Yes, Tanya, I can live with that price, if—"

Before Diamond could finish the sentence, Tanya said, "I will address the rest of your question after Mr. Goldberg approves his end.

Our offer is two million dollars for unit 705. Is that acceptable, Mr. Goldberg?"

The three men nodded. No one said a word, as they eyed the suitcases.

CHAPTER TWENTY-SIX
MONEY TALKS

Tanya wheeled over the closest case, unlocked the clasp, and unzipped the cover. Wrapped inside were stacks of hundred-dollar bills assembled in perfect order, Each stack was taped with a sticker announcing the contents were twenty thousand dollars. Taub ran his fingers across the money, lifting the top stack to find the same, row upon row. All four board members, men accustomed to dealing in large sums, usually by check or wire transfer, were mesmerized.

"The other suitcase filled like this one, Tanya?" Taub asked.

"Yes, Mr. Taub. Last week I told you this would be a cash deal, and I meant it. I have a packet for each of you containing a bill of sale for far less money than we just agreed upon. That should answer your earlier question, which referred to capital gains taxes. A wire transfer to your financial institutions in an amount slightly higher than your original purchase price goes out when you sign the deal. The rest will be paid under the table in cash to give the appearance of a legitimate real-estate transaction. I wanted you to see the cash to verify I represent a serious buyer. I'm going to the ladies' room. You folks can have a chat in my absence."

Tanya stood and headed to one of Taub's bathrooms. Taub yelled after her, "Tanya, are you leaving the money here? Suppose we walk away with it?"

"You won't do such a thing, gentlemen. Grigori's *Spetsnaz* security wouldn't let you leave the building. We know you are Jews. As Jews, you're familiar with the reputation of the Israeli Mossad. If you believe, as I do, those agents are nothing to fool around with, then imagine the Mossad as choirboys compared with the *Spetsnaz*."

Rabinowitz, stone silent until now since he wasn't selling a unit, just looking out for the other owners' interest, said, "When she comes back, I want to hear what she has to say about Grozny. I don't care if she's carrying Fort Knox in those satchels. If Tanya or Grigori and Daddy are Muslims, I'm not going along with this deal. They can fly to hell on their prayer mats."

"OK, Stu. We know where you stand. What about you, Izzy?"

Diamond said, "Muslim, shmuslim. If I can walk away with my pockets stuffed with cash, I don't care if they're from the Ku Klux Klan. Money is money. I'll get in on the new condos being built down the road, the place where the entire floor is one apartment. I can pay cash and be done with mortgages and interest for the rest of my life. I say take the money. We won't be getting a better offer today."

Tanya returned to her place and settled in, taking pains to display her legs.

"Well, gentlemen. What's the verdict?"

CHAPTER TWENTY-SEVEN

MUSLIMS?

Rabinowitz's face revealed a dislike for Tanya. He said, "Your hometown, Grozny, is a nest of Muslims. Those people have been at war with Russia since 1990. At one point, the Russians lost more tanks in mountain battles than they lost in the entire battle for Berlin. The rebels have fought the Russians using terrorism tactics. Do you remember when the rebels invaded a grade school. The attack lasted three days and ended with the deaths of over three hundred people, including many children. I don't want their kind here. Convince me you and Grigori are not Muslim."

Tanya threw back her head and laughed at Rabinowitz. Tanya spoke directly to him from strength. She knew the questions and challenge were coming.

"Muslim? Look at me, Mr. Rabinowitz. I was raised in an Orthodox church. To this day, Grigori and I are parishioners at St. Vladimir's Catholic Church on Front Street in Hempstead."

Tanya stood and walked over to Rabinowitz. She opened the top buttons on her blouse and pulled out a silver chain carrying a cross. She dangled it in front of Rabinowitz's face.

"Muslims don't wear crosses, Mr. Rabinowitz," Tanya said. "I'm deeply offended by your accusation. Chechen rebels have committed atrocities to make the Nazi invaders look like children at play. If you don't want the deal, we'll take our bags of cash down the road. Remember, money talks and bullshit walks."

Still standing, Tanya turned her wrath on the other board members. "Mr. Taub. You've had our offer. Take it or leave it."

Tanya zippered the open suitcase, blocking out the money. She locked it and said, "*Das Sveedaneeya*, men. That's Russian for good-bye." She grabbed both handles and wheeled her cash fortune to the elevator.

Rabinowitz, terrified he had just killed a lucrative deal for his friends, chased after Tanya. "Don't go," he shouted. "I was talking out loud. You've convinced me you don't represent terrorists. I was out of line, and I apologize. Please don't kill the deal because of my big mouth."

Goldberg added, "Tanya, Stu was way out of line. Don't let his prejudices ruin a good deal for everyone. I think I can speak for the board. We're unanimous in going ahead with the sales and improvements, except for the helicopter pad on the roof. Do you want to pass around the contracts and bills of sale? We want to send the paperwork to our lawyers."

Tanya returned to her place and removed manila envelopes from her bag. She handed them to the parties of interest. "Take note of the fact that I wrote in a sale price to minimize capital gains. As I mentioned before, when the deal is ready, each of you will get the remainder in cash, as you saw it in my suitcases."

Tanya grabbed her suitcases, wheeled them to the elevator and waved good-bye saying, "I want to expedite the sales. So have your lawyers drop what they're doing and get on this. Let them know, they'll be well compensated for their time."

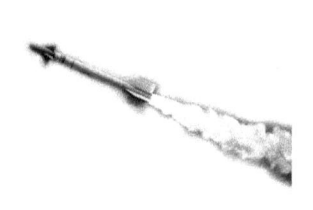

CHAPTER TWENTY-EIGHT
MOVING DAY

May 14

Tanya had fast tracked the purchase of units 705, 805, and 806. Deeds, titles, wire transfers, and satchels stuffed with hundred-dollar bills exchanged hands.

Sellers agreed to vacate the units by Saturday, May 14. The Aqua rules allow moves to take place Monday through Friday, 8:00 a.m. to 4:00 p.m. To speed things up, wads of money in unmarked envelopes found their way into Jules Goldberg's hands. General Stankovich rode his blue-and-white bicycle down Lincoln Boulevard to inspect the sellers' progress. He grunted in satisfaction as moving vans loaded away cardboard boxes and furniture. Trucks, sellers, and money departed Long Beach for parts unknown. The general pedaled to a prearranged meeting point and picked out a familiar olive green Range Rover.

Dismounting and hopping into the front seat, the general said, "Grigori, three trucks have hauled away the sellers' junk. The movers did the job in record time."

"*Da,* General. We threw in extra dollars for the movers to come ahead of time and prepackage everything in boxes. What you saw was an express train running from unit to truck. We wanted no delay. I have the fob, and we will move in tomorrow. Our people will bring up beds and mattresses, dishes and utensils. By nightfall, one Grinch launcher and missile will be in a spare bedroom. The other goes upstate to Roscoe. Suicide vests for the *shahida* will be taken to the safe house."

"Why you, Grigori? How come Tanya isn't helping move the weapons?"

"There isn't enough room for her after I lower the seats to make space for the canisters. It wouldn't do for Tanya to sit on top of a rocket. She does enough by sitting on top of O'Leary and Hoffman. After dispersing the arsenal, Tanya and I will pick up O'Leary at Killenworth. We'll use a step van to keep him out of sight."

"Good. I'm pleased with the work, Grigori. On a personal note, my thanks for eliminating Oleg. He wasn't up to the mission and may have folded on us. He had to go."

"I know, General. He's one problem we don't have to deal with."

"*Da*, Grigori. Eliminate your problems before they fester into disasters. Carry on."

"*Da*, the thunderstorms proved to be a boon for the mission. Downpours guarantee a deserted beach. That is, everyone but the surfers. Regardless of the weather, after a camera check, they ride the waves. Thunderstorms are mother's milk to surfers. The rougher the waves, the more they like it," Grigori said.

"I like them. They have balls," Stankovich said.

Late Saturday night, Grigori drove to the defunct auto repair shop. Following a set routine, he unlocked the gate, opened the bay door and parked inside. After backing the Rover to the vault, he hit the automatic rear hatch opener and flattened the seats.

CHAPTER TWENTY-NINE

WEAPONS OF MASS DESTRUCTION

Grigori got straight to business, packing up the Grinches, then the missiles. Satisfied, he carefully nestled two explosive-packed boxes in between the rocket launchers. Garment bags toting the suicide vests were draped over the ordnance. Blankets covered the weapons.

Surveying his work, he noted a small depression in the earth which was to be expected. Grigori had a final thought: *Let me check on Oleg's grave. Settling of the dirt. Nothing appears to be amiss.*

Driving off in the rain, Grigori returned to Long Beach and pulled the Rover into the underground parking garage. He didn't notice that the surfers' pan-tilt and zoom camera was moving about, sending images of crashing waves. Grigori ignored several *Spetsnaz* moving men and went to unit 805 by private elevator.

"Welcome home, Grigori," Tanya said. Sitting in the kitchen was General Stankovich who produced a bottle of Stolichnaya Russian vodka and three glasses.

"Work is done. Now is a good time to celebrate. We are down to fifty-four days to initiate Operation Russian *Revansh*."

Stankovich filled the glasses, threw back his head, and swallowed two shots of vodka. Before Tanya and Grigori could take a drink, the general said, "*Nostrovia*—cheers."

Tanya and Grigori drank to please the general. They took short sips and replied, "*Nostrovia.*"

Stankovich refilled his glass with three shots. "Now, a full report and leave nothing out."

Tanya spoke first. "Late tonight, O'Leary will arrive. Another yellow arrow has been painted on his bedroom wall to show him the direction of Mecca. When Russian *Revansh* is completed, the Americans will find the arrow and black flag, leaving a clue for the authorities. I will make love to O'Leary under the ISIS flag in his new bed. I intend to keep him at peace for fifty-four days."

"Good, Tanya. Your turn, Grigori."

"I'm off to the Roscoe safe house. Qahira and Malak's vests and explosives will be stored securely. Qahira has been trained to smuggle explosives into her locker at Citi Field in small amounts. On July eighth, she will enter martyrdom. Malak doesn't have to be so elaborate. She will arrive at the synagogue ready to go."

"That leaves the other Grinch. What's the plan?"

"As soon as the safe house transfer is complete, I'll be off to Roscoe. The second Grinch and missile stored in a woodshed. On July eighth, our transport vehicle will take Hoffman to LaGuardia Airport."

"What kind of transport?"

"We have removed the roof of a small van and replaced it with canvas. At the right time, the canvas will be unrolled leaving Hoffman an unobstructed shot as his target. The pieces of the puzzle are in place. Our security people and drivers have been handpicked. They are dedicated to the mission."

With that, Stankovich poured himself a third large vodka, swigged it down and said, "I'm back to my bike and out of here. The less I'm seen, the better. Another drink, comrades?"

Tanya and Grigori declined.

Stankovich smiled, capped his vodka and stuffed it into his backpack. He hit the elevator button and was gone.

"Tanya," Grigori said, "we're lucky to serve under a brilliant man. The general has approved everything down to the smallest detail."

Tanya sucked in a deep breath and shook her head. "Grigori, he knew the answer to his questions before we opened our mouths. General Stankovich may like his vodka, but he's also a master chess player. That man is ten moves ahead of us. If they ever make a movie about Adam and Eve, the general would be perfect to play the serpent. Don't forget. Let's go to Killenworth as soon as it gets dark. The weatherman says it will still be raining."

CHAPTER THIRTY

MARTYRDOM VIDEO

O'Leary, AKA Ahmed, was waiting in his cell, fidgeting with his thumbs and hands clasped.

"Is everything all right?" Tanya said.

"No. I want to redo my martyrdom video. There's more to be said about America."

"I think your video is well done," Tanya said. "There's no need to modify the words. It's short and to the point, Ahmed. What do you want to add?"

He handed her a sheet of paper. In block lettering, Ahmed had written:

> Think not of those who are slain in Allah's way as dead. Nay, they live, finding their way in the sustenance of their Lord. They rejoice in the bounty provided by Allah. And with regard to those left behind, on them is no fear. They have no cause to grieve. There is no God but *Allahu*. He has ordained the destruction of the Great Satan, America. We have crossed the ocean. My assault on the airplane was the first bullet in a war against the infidels. Hellfire is waiting for all Americans. Those who refuse to convert to Islam and adopt Sharia law will be destroyed. My surviving ISIS

brothers will see to the creation of a caliphate in the godless America. Long live ISIS. *Allahu Akbar.*

Tanya returned the paper to her assassin.
"That's strong language, Ahmed. I have no objection to your new speech. I would prefer you memorize the words and speak directly to the camera from the heart."

BOOK FOUR

Policemen are often confronted with situations which baffle them at first. A certain crime scene may seem meaningless, but they have to derive some meaning out of it. They have to connect the dots, find the links, delve into its history, look for evidence, come up with a zillion theories, and arrive at truth. The thing is, truth is always stranger than fiction.

Mahendra Jakhar
The Butcher of Benares

CHAPTER THIRTY-ONE

CRIME-SCENE INVESTIGATION

May 16

From two long blocks, I spotted yellow-and-black crime-scene tape strung around the building. A kaleidoscope of flashing red and blue lights mounted atop white police cruisers dressed up an otherwise rundown factory-residential district. Coventry Road was not part of Long Island's fabled Gold Coast. Clapboard houses surrounding decrepit factories produced a hungry crowd of spectators. Drawing near, I picked out crime-scene techs and Emergency Services cops on the grounds. Someone had produced a set of bolt cutters to sever the gate's lock and chain. Caesar and his handler were in the side rear yard. Crime-scene techs were photographing, measuring, and drawing a diagram. ESU men waited along the fence line armed with shovels, spades, tarpaulins, and canvas slings. I had an image of lurking medieval grave robbers waiting for the sun to set. Crowds of goggle-eyed civilians gathered in knots and whispered to one another, speculating on the fate of the person on the wrong side of the yellow tape. As I took it in, a black unmarked morgue van known in police lingo as the 'meat wagon' arrived. A hush came over the crowd.

O.J. Simpson's infamous trial had turned murder into show business. Rubberneckers don't want to meet a survivor. They linger until a murdered body shrouded in a body bag is wheeled out on a gurney. Secretly, they pray for the bag to burst open and spill bloody, mutilated contents onto the road. Cell phone pictures document the show and stream across the Internet spreading joy to those who can't attend the spectacle. Crowds, reporters, and the meat wagon at a murder scene blend like scotch and soda. They mix well like props in a Broadway play. Lights, cameras, action. Front row, center seat for bored blood-thirsty ghouls who can't get enough.

Trained by television's *CSI*, the throngs understand what homicide detectives have down pat. Murders are like snowflakes. No two are identical. Everyone wants to be in on a fresh story, an oddball characteristic, a thriller with a lurid sex angle, evidence of either infidelity or lust. In the meantime, the masses wait for the meat wagon to accept its grisly cargo, once a thriving human being, loved and loving, reduced to roadkill.

Parking my Crown Victoria illegally—on the wrong side of the road under a no-parking sign—is a calculated gamble. Who the hell is going to slap a ticket on the official car assigned to me, the Homicide South commander? I grabbed my briefcase and headed to say hello to a new acquaintance, homicide number 27, behind the tape. Walking along the sidewalk, a loudmouth said to no one in particular, "Who is she? I had to park a block away. She must be connected."

I pivoted, returned to the Crown Vic, and dug a cardboard sign out of the glove compartment. I placed it upright on the dashboard. The placard read,

OFFICIAL BUSINESS
COMMANDING OFFICER
HOMICIDE SQUAD SOUTH

I aimed my green eyes at the complainer who hung his head and slinked off.

My custom is to look over the scene, make mental notes, and then go sniff out the body. I mean that literally. Heat and moisture whip up a special brew that surrounds dead bodies with god-awful stinks. Processing a murder scene is a tedious task—multiple interviews, photographs, measurements, a background check on the victim, and I never seem to have enough people to do it all. In this case, I waited for Crime Scene to finish and was glad to see the arrival of two comrades: homicide bureau chief, assistant district attorney Joshua Hirsch and deputy medical examiner Astrid Ludwig rounded out the team.

We met outside the fence and reinforced an old law-enforcement routine, shaking hands as if meeting for the first time, although we have known each other for years. The Homicide South team pulled up and copied the routine. I filled everyone in on the sketchy details and consulted with Crime Scene who were wrapping up exterior shots. Then I went behind the building to examine a patch of ground doubling as a grave site. The surrounding earth, littered with rocks and oil-stained debris, stood in marked contrast to Caesar's discovery. The top layer, clean with fresh weeds fertilized by a decomposing body, gave it an unnaturally pristine appearance compared with the rest of the yard.

"Dig it up, men," I said. "Let's hope it isn't a bloody gooey mess. When you get it out, lay it on a tarp. We'll examine it and then ship it to the morgue."

I wanted to confirm Tom Clark's so-called bloodstain and shell casings while the grave robbers went about their business.

"Frank," I said, "take Horton, Morgan, and a crime-scene tech to verify Officer Clark's blood-stain observations. Don't worry about a search warrant. The stuff we want to eyeball is lying out in open view."

Sergeant DiGregorio directed Detectives Taylor Morgan and Ron Horton to climb through the pried open window. "I'm no longer an athlete," he told them. "When you get in, open the front door for me. Give an old sarge a break."

In spite of my warning to Clark—"Don't get caught by news cameras chuckling it up at a murder scene." I laughed out loud, then covered my mouth. I went behind the building to stifle the image of DiGregorio's fifty-inch waist playing Burglar Frank. Overhearing my snickering, Frank looked at me. He displayed his palms upward in mock surrender.

"Boss," he said, "sometimes you gotta recognize your limitations."

"Well said, Frank. My Irish cousin, Teresa Walsh, would say, 'Sure he has an arse the size of a brewery horse. He'll never make it through the window.' Make your grand entrance while I supervise the exhumation."

CHAPTER THIRTY-TWO
EXHUMATION

Caesar, leashed to his handler, watched patiently with Detectives Kowalsky and Cassidy, ADA Hirsch and Dr. Ludwig. It was evident the grave diggers weren't making their debut at exhuming a decomposing body. They knew their business. Most men would spear the earth with spades and toss the contents helter-skelter. Not these guys. Caesar's nose had found a murder victim. ESU guys know the body is a critical piece of evidence to be handled with kid gloves. They carried out the dig with a disciplined, archaeological protocol.

Spades probed the soft earth until metal struck something nature hadn't placed in the hole. The diggers skimmed layers of earth. As they scraped away at the surface, my sense of smell was assaulted by the rancid unmistakable odor of a rotting corpse as the outline of a human body was exposed. ESU men put their spades aside and replaced them with brooms for light sweeping. Damp, dark earth, now mostly scraped away, confirmed the worst. There he was, a fully clothed white man, lying face down in a makeshift grave behind a decrepit auto-repair shop. A crunched Panama hat and Ray-Ban sunglasses lay on his back.

A vial of Vicks VapoRub found its way into my left palm. Two dabs, placed under each nostril, ensured suppressing a noxious stink like an open cesspool. It was necessary. First, I am the Homicide

Squad South commander, and it just wouldn't do to vomit all over a crime scene. Second, and more important, I labor in a white male environment where, for the most part, members of my gender remain unwelcome. Reports of Lieutenant McAvoy vomiting all over a crime scene would go viral, confirming what everyone suspected: "See, she can't handle it. McAvoy's just another affirmative action face in the table of organization. Diversity, not experience, is the order of the day."

I had heard it all from day one in the police academy. After graduation, I was partnered up with Alexandra Cameron, a six-foot-tall African-American woman from the previous class of recruits. I began police life with another rookie. We figured out the reason for our partnership was a setup for failure. "Two women can't handle the job as well as one man. Throw them in the deep end of the pool and let 'em drown." Lex's sin was her race, and mine was being the daughter of the head of Internal Affairs. What they didn't know and their prejudices had blocked out was that Lex and I were two sharp cookies. Instead of drowning, we excelled. Police work is 90 percent mental and 10 percent physical. We used our wits and feminine guile to overcome confrontations where a male officer might have resorted to violence. Within a year of failing to disappoint the misogynists, we earned the nicknames Annie Oakley and Calamity Jane.

Since I don't get paid for excavating old memories. I turned to the job at hand, excavating a decomposing murder victim instead. In order to avoid having the body turn into a bowl of gelatin, the ESU cops slipped sets of canvas slings under the body. Each man knelt at the edge of the open trench and snaked slings under the corpse. Three slings in all—one under the upper torso, belly, and legs guaranteed the body came out of the ground intact.

Blue tarpaulin, laid out like a dining-room tablecloth, straddled the side of the grave, waiting for a body. Each man grabbed a loose end of a sling. Kowalsky and Cassidy took the leg sling.

"On the count of three, lift and drop," an ESU sergeant announced.

Lifters steadied their feet at the edge of the grave. Six hefty men hauling up a corpse could easily collapse a wall of the trench, leaving several cops spilling into the quagmire.

"One, two, three," yelled the ESU sergeant.

In unison, three slings hoisted the body. Carrying the corpse like delicate China, it was laid face down on the tarp.

The slings were pulled out from under the body and set aside. The grave diggers stepped away to allow Dr. Ludwig the first examination. As she snapped on latex gloves, Dr. Ludwig checked her watch. "Time of pronouncement is eleven forty-five a.m."

Straddling the body, she bent to examine the head. Poking her index finger into his hair, she said, "I think I see two entry wounds at the back of the skull. There may be more. His hair is matted down with dirt and moisture. Skin slippage peeling off the body allows me to guesstimate he's been dead for a while, two to four weeks, give or take. We'll know a lot more after an autopsy, which I've scheduled for tomorrow morning."

Moving the corpse's head from side to side, Dr. Ludwig said, "He could be early middle age. Are there any questions?"

CHAPTER THIRTY-THREE
IDENTIFICATION

"Not now, Doc," I said. "I'd like to turn my team loose to search the guy. Looks like a fat wallet in the back pocket."

"OK with me," Dr. Ludwig said. "Good hunting."

Kowalsky and Cassidy took their time snapping on latex gloves. Searching a decomposed body is a morbid business, not to be rushed.

"Expensive clothing on the guy," I said to Kowalsky.

"Yeah, boss. This guy was no factory worker. His rags are worth more than anything I own. Looks like a Rolex watch and a diamond pinky ring on his left hand. Do you think they're real?" he asked.

Finding a clean corner of the tarp, I set my knees down for a closer look. "Let's take a look at the bling. I know a thing or two about Rolex knockoffs and diamonds."

Lifting homicide number twenty-seven's left arm, I found the Rolex to be ticking. "Check out the second hand, Bob. A knockoff stops every second, tick-tock. True Rolexes are equipped with a sweeping unbroken second hand. This one is moving nonstop around the dial."

I pried a thin gold pinky ring from his left joint. Peering inside, I saw a 14k mark certifying it was real gold. Alongside the mark, two sets of initials were visible: *OP & KA*. "If the gold is real, the diamonds are most likely authentic also. Get a bag for this stuff and pull out the wallet."

Kowalsky returned with an evidence bag, unlocked the watch and flipped it over. "Looks like our boy is Oleg and he got the Swiss timepiece from Karen. 'All my love,' it says."

"I'll dig out the wallet to see if his paperwork matches the initials O.P.," Kowalsky added.

Fiddling with the pocket button, Kowalsky retrieved a leather wallet which had absorbed the wretched odor of decomposition. Undeterred, Kowalsky spread out the wallet contents, laying them on the tarp.

Over his shoulder, I saw a substantial amount of cash and a pack of credit cards. "How much money is there?"

"Fast count comes to six hundred thirty-five dollars. I see ten credit cards in the name of Oleg Petrovsky and a company-issued ID card. The company is Security First with a Brighton Beach address. I don't see either a driver's license or a social security card. There's a photo of a man and a woman holding hands. The back side says Karen and Oleg, 2014."

Kowalsky fingered through smudged, wet, rancid paperwork.

"Bingo, boss. Here's a business card for Karen Arkady. She lives in Fair Lawn, New Jersey. According to the card, she's a concert violinist for the New York Philharmonic."

"Roll him over, Bob," I said. "Cassidy, help out. I don't want Oleg to come apart."

The detectives did as they were told. Oleg's body, face up on the tarp, bore a strong resemblance to the man in the snapshot.

"I'm opening a machine copy of Oleg's passport. Our boy is a Russian citizen. His date of birth is February 9, 1972," Bob said, handing me the document.

"So, we have a forty-four-year-old Russian national, executed gangland style in back of a junkyard auto-repair shop, wearing expensive jewelry and clothing, and carrying enough cash to keep a heroin addict high for a week. Let's put robbery on the back burner for now," I said. Examining the passport photo, I came up with a couple of ideas to move the investigation away from the filthy yard.

CHAPTER THIRTY-FOUR

CRIME SCENE NUMBER TWO

A sharp knock sounding on the steel back door broke my concentration.

"Is it okay to open the door?" Frank's muffled voice asked.

I told him, "Join the wake, Frank. We're getting to know a few things about our dead boy and his lady fair. Turns out he's a Russian named Oleg Petrovsky, running around with a concert violinist. Looks like this case will be taking us out of Westbury and into the streets of Manhattan and New Jersey."

Frank stepped into the yard and circled the tarp. Before sticking his thumbs into his belt loops, the sergeant ran a comb through his hair. Balding, he had reverted to a comb over. Vanity, and the possibility of showing up on the six o'clock news, prompted him to work the hair.

"Boss," he said, "we found two cartridge cases from a forty-caliber Glock. They may have identifiable fingerprints. While you were busy with our friend Oleg, I asked the highway cop to allow Caesar to check out the joint, just to be on the safe side. He didn't find another body, but it appears there's a false wall hiding a room running parallel to the rear yard. The cop tells me Caesar's not acting like there's another body, but the dog smells something. The handler suggested I put in a call for highway's other specialist dogs, one for drugs and the other an explosive-detection sniffer. I did just that, and they're on the way."

Patience, Patti, I told myself. Working a variety of murder cases has trained me to wait. Wait for the D.A. Wait for the M.E. Wait for a search warrant. Wait for the results of a polygraph. Wait for the lab results. And now, I wait for dogs.

Pacing the repair-shop bay allowed me to escape with dignity from Oleg's stench. Crime-scene techs methodically took blood samples and photographs. In my mind, I reconstructed the murder. Oleg took the hit, bang-bang, and fell forward flat on his face. From there, he was dragged out the back door like a heavy carpet and dumped in the hole like yesterday's garbage.

I said to Frank, "One shooter, one dragger. If there were two, we wouldn't have a red smear of a blood trail. Each would have carried an end."

"Let's not rule out another player who didn't want to dirty his hands. Keep your options and your mind open, boss," Frank said. "C'mon, take a gander at the wall."

Frank pointed to a small metal track, a groove like the one used in sliding bathroom shower doors. "The wall slides along the track and reaches a point where it overlaps the rest of the wall. We found a numeric matrix keypad device—twelve buttons arranged in a telephone grid. Punch in the password, like your ATM PIN code, and the wall slides open. The pad is hidden in the electric panel power box alongside circuit breakers."

Frank popped the aluminum power box cover revealing the usual circuit breakers. Hardly noticeable, a keypad was attached to a side of the box.

Red flags flew all through my brain.

"Frank," I said, "without fanfare, shut down the scenes and evacuate everyone, including the spectators, to a block away. I'm going to err on the side of caution and assume there may be explosives on the other side of the door. Do it now."

Before *now* hit his ear, Frank was on the move. He moved fast for a big man, like a grizzly bear on the scent. He quickly emptied both crime scenes. Rounding up the uniform cops, Frank instructed them to move the civilians onto the next block.

Frank turned to me and whispered, "I'm calling out the bomb squad, just in case."

I nodded. "Thanks for watching my back, Frank. Get on the horn."

CHAPTER THIRTY-FIVE

K-9 Dogs

On cue, two Highway Patrol cops and their German shepherd dogs arrived. First on the scene was a hundred-pound shepherd. She looked like an extra from a prison-escape movie. I met the handler, told him about our suspicions, and asked him to volunteer. I wouldn't order him into the building.

"Lieutenant," he said, "we only use alpha dogs for this kind of work. Casey is a drug sniffer. That's all she does. We like to keep the dogs focused on one target. Casey looks for pot, crack, cocaine, meth, and heroin, among other things. If drug contraband is in the building, she'll find it. It's what we do," the cop said.

Casey and the cop went through the building and returned to the road. "She found nothing," he said.

I met up with the next cop who introduced me to another German shepherd the size of a small pony. Her pointed ears, raised like pennants, complemented her nose, which was designed by nature to sniff out the faintest odors. It missed nothing. "Sheba's an explosives-detection canine. EDC's, we call them," the cop said, "Like Casey, she's highly trained. Her expertise is explosives running the range from TNT, C-4, Semtex, dynamite, PETN, ammonium nitrate, and black-powder fuses to name a few. She's been introduced to the new ISIS toy, TATP, known as the 'witches brew'. TATP is made from hydrogen peroxide and acetone, stuff you can buy in a drugstore. It smells like bleach. Sheba had to be retrained to recognize the new technology of death. TATP is the explosive terrorists used in the Brussels airport. If she's on to something, she'll sit. That's her alert signal."

I gave Sheba's handler the same option as Casey's. "I won't order you to go in the building. It's your call, officer. I'll go with you, if you prefer."

"Glad to have your help. Let's go, Lieutenant."

Sheba and her handler traversed the interior, going from room to room. Heading toward the back door, Sheba towed the cop who had to pull hard on the black leash. "She's in what we call four-paw overdrive because she's onto something," the cop said. Sheba halted and sat in the alert position facing the wall.

"She's found something on or behind the wall," he announced.

"No mistake, Officer?" I asked.

"None, Lieutenant. Sheba can find a firecracker in the Empire State Building. Take it to the bank."

"All right, Officer. Thanks for being a stand-up guy. It's good to work with alpha dogs and alpha cops. Wait outside with the others," I said.

I followed Sheba and the cop to the road and spotted Frank with his head in a bomb-squad explosives truck's window. I was pleased to see the bomb-squad guy join us and none too soon. Waving for Detective Kowalsky and ADA Hirsch, I invited them to an impromptu staff meeting. After updating the pair on Sheba's discovery, I turned to Joshua Hirsch for legal advice.

"Josh," I asked, "search warrant?"

"Yeah," he said, "based on the circumstances and the magnitude of the crime, I'll ask for an oral warrant like we do in drunk-driving cases. The duty judge is Hardigan. He loves homicide and would authorize you guys to storm the gates of heaven. Besides, paperwork and affidavits may take all night. We don't have that kind of time."

"Before we move too fast, I have a suggestion," Bomb-squad detective Bob Rafferty said.

He swung open the rear doors of the explosive truck and said, "Meet my little buddy, Apple Annie, the robot."

Instantly, I grasped the meaning of the 'suggestion.' The door may be booby-trapped. The robot is expendable. Detectives like Rafferty are not.

"What's the plan, Rafferty?"

"Annie can go behind the building, drill a hole through the cinder block and sheetrock. I'll insert a pinhole spy camera and scan the room. If a trap has been rigged, we'll spot the explosives and triggering device. If not, we go to plan B."

"And that is what?" I asked

"What we do best. Take down the door."

"Do it, Rafferty."

Unexpectedly, he threw a challenge at me. "Care to join me, Lieutenant?"

My pause was imperceptible. "Rafferty, let's take your girlfriend Annie on a triple date."

Rafferty and I, along with his "little girl," went around the building. Halfway there, I heard the familiar whir of helicopter blades. Cablevision's blue and yellow eye-in-the-sky hovered, recording the episode for the five-o'clock news cycle known as *Night Side*. It was too good for the pilot and reporter to pass up. A scene of cops, detectives, evacuations, dogs, and a bomb detection robot are red meat for newscasters. The downside for me was that the police brass would also be watching and have a million questions. I promised myself to make a few calls to the bosses as soon as Rafferty told me the building was clear. In the meantime, I threw my purse over my shoulder and followed Apple Annie.

Along the way, a to-do list formed in my mind dominated by one question. What the hell is a well-dressed Russian national doing with a couple of bullets in his brain in an unmarked Westbury grave alongside a room of explosives?

The question would dominate my life for the duration of the investigation.

CHAPTER THIRTY-SIX

SEARCH WARRANT

Working Oleg's murder scene, I overheard ADA Joshua Hirsch call the search warrant duty Judge Hardigan. Partnering with a competent ADA always gives me a sense of pride as a player in the police, medical, and legal team dedicated to catching the bad guys.

Shutting off his phone, Hirsch grabbed a seat in the bomb-disposal truck and took out his iPad. Typing up an application for an oral search warrant would baffle most in the law-enforcement game. Hirsch handled the job like he was making out a food shopping list. His fingers flew across the keys. Within minutes, he hit the send button and did what we do best at murder scenes—he waited. The entire apparatus of Nassau County's criminal justice system waited for a chirp from a little black box lying on the front seat of Detective Rafferty's bomb-explosives truck.

Except for the news chopper, the area was silent. Somehow, the chopper pilot sensed we were waiting for important news. He drifted in circles, then hovered like the vulture in my office, and waited like the rest of us.

I couldn't wait any longer and buried myself in my police car. Cigarettes are truly an addiction, and I desperately needed a nicotine hit. My body demanded the drug, and I, of no will, succumbed to the temptation. As soon as my butt hit the seat, I lit up a Parliament 100. *Jesus*, I thought, *a glass of cold Pinot Grigio would go down nice.*

I pulled down the sun visors to hide from the helicopter. No good. He was all over me. The pilot dropped to treetop level and hovered at a low angle photographing me smoking at a crime scene. What the hell? If that's all to go wrong today, I'll consider it a good day.

As an afterthought, I called the Public Information Office and filled in the clerk with sketchy details. I knew my dispatch would trigger a round of calls to the local reporters, and they would arrive posthaste.

My rearview mirror came alive with moving bodies. Hirsch picked up his chirping iPad. We made eye contact, and he raised his right thumb upward. We were in business. I approved Rafferty's plan to take down the door, but I like to do it with the full force of the law in my pocket.

As I got out of my car, I stood in the roadway and made a circular motion with my arm, our signal to gather around.

Hirsch spoke first. "You have your search warrant. Hardigan added a no-knock authorization. You may blow up the door with his authority. No pun intended."

I smiled. Everyone in the homicide game develops a gallows sense of humor.

CHAPTER THIRTY-SEVEN

PEEK FIRST, THEN SEARCH

"Rafferty!" I yelled. "Get your operating tools from the truck. Drill me a hole so we can look inside the vault."

"Yes, boss," he said, climbing into the box truck.

Rafferty piled two boxes at the rear door and bounded into the street like a kid on a trampoline. He was armed with the tools of his trade—a portable drill, a backup battery, and several drill bits, each one a foot or more in length.

"What's in the other box, Rafferty?" I said, pointing to a small suitcase.

"That's my gooseneck pinhole camera. Don't be fooled by its size. Tiny it may be, the lens captures high-resolution video and connects to Annie's monitor. Even in a low-light room, I'll get a picture of what is or isn't in the vault."

"OK, Raff, show me."

I circled the building with the bomb-squad expert. He moved Annie into position, inserted a bit into the drill, and chocked it into place. He looked like a dentist about to drill a cavity without the use of Novocain.

Rafferty's bit punched a hole through porous cinder block. He paused when he felt resistance as the bit bored through a two-by-four support beam and Sheetrock.

"I'm in," Rafferty said, putting his gooseneck together. The hole he made had the diameter of his camera, and he fed the device through the wall. It had the look of a tailor threading the eye of a needle.

Attaching a manual control joystick to his end, an image popped up on Annie's monitor.

"Boss, I see two empty picnic tables and nothing else. I'm on the door, and it looks clean to me. No booby-traps or suspicious devices. I say go ahead," Rafferty said.

Just then, the nosy noisy chopper got close. Whipping winds from the chopper's blades lifted my skirt. Pointing at the pilot with my right index finger, I mouthed, "Back off!" He got the message and retreated to the tree line.

CHAPTER THIRTY-EIGHT

TAKING DOWN THE DOOR

I looked around to catch the team watching Rafferty and Annie doing their bit for police work. Sergeant DiGregorio, and Detectives Kowalsky, Horton, Morgan, and Cassidy waited for instructions.

"We don't have all day to break the Enigma code controlling the door panel. Kowalsky, have the Emergency Service guys pry it open with crowbars," I said.

"How about the Jaws of Life?" Kowalsky said.

"If they have it, turn 'em loose."

Within minutes, the professional ESU crew carried the Jaws of Life.

I asked the sergeant in charge of the ESU, "How does the thing work?"

"Well, Lieutenant," he said, "Jaws' real name is a Hurst Rescue Tool. It was invented to pull race-car drivers out of severe crashes. The jaws use cutters, spreaders or rams. In our case, I'm going to use the spreader. We wedge a tip into the door-frame seam like a car door and force it open. The work is done by a hydraulic pump powered by a piston. This baby uses ten thousand pounds per square inch. As a point of reference, it only takes four psi to extinguish a cigarette butt."

I backed off while the Jaws were spreading apart the steel door from its mooring. Jaws demolished the door like a weightlifting drunk crushing a beer can. The door was spread open a yard wide when I called for the dog.

"Bring Sheba in," I ordered and watched a nine-thousand-dollar police dog earn her pay.

Sheba patrolled the ten-by-twenty-foot room, the size of a suburban one-car garage. She sat alert at each picnic table. Her handler rewarded the dog with a treat, and they hugged the walls. At a wall opposite the broken door, Sheba sat in the alert position. Not visible to the naked eye, Sheba pointed her snout at minuscule white flakes no more than the size of dust particles.

"No way I would have spotted them," I said. "The county got a good return on its investment."

Motioning for the forensics team, I took a position by the door to allow room for the experts to gather trace evidence.

I took Sheba's handler aside. His name tag read "Harper, Jr."

"I worked with your father, Sam, back in the day. Good detective. We called him 'the Hunter.' It's apparent the apple didn't fall far from the tree. Good job, Harper. What do you think our little snowflakes are?"

"If I had to lay a bet, I'd go for C-4 on this one. Common military explosive. Not hard to get," Harper said.

"What about the tables?" I asked. "Just an odor? Same thing as Sheba found on the floor?"

"No. Something big was planted on the tables. The flakes fell off something hanging near the wall. I'm thinking bombs or some other type of explosive device was married to the tables."

"Well, I'll defer to your expertise, Harper. I have a sense of foreboding suggesting your bombs found their way into a derelict auto to be converted into a suicide car bomb."

"Jesus, Lieutenant. You think outside of the box."

"That's what they pay me to do. Thanks for all your help. Give your dad a big hello from me."

CHAPTER THIRTY-NINE

TRACE EVIDENCE

Frank DiGregorio was moving fast, carrying an open iPad. Trailing behind his fast-moving legs was a forensics detective half his age.

"What's up, Frank? You're beaming like a lottery winner. What news have you got in your right paw?"

"Boss, in the homicide game, sometimes the gods smile and throw us dogs a bone."

"Frank, is there meat on my bone?"

"Enough for a Thanksgiving dinner, boss. Remember I told you we found fingerprints on the ejected cartridges?"

Nodding to the forensics detective, I asked, "What have you got for me, Cheryl?"

"I snapped photos of the prints and ran them through the local, state, and federal data bases. We got a positive hit on a thirty-year-old Russian named Grigori Glinka. He was nabbed at a DWI checkpoint six years ago, arrested, posted a thousand-dollar bond, and skipped out on his court appearances. There's an active bench warrant for our boy Glinka."

"Can I have a picture, Cheryl?"

"On its way, boss. I asked the photo section to produce a collection of eight-by-tens of the comrade," Frank said.

"What's with the 'comrade'?"

"Grigori and Oleg are Russian nationals. They call each other comrade in that country."

"Yeah, I get it. So far, we have Oleg from Brighton Beach, Grigori and Karen from Fair Lawn, New Jersey."

"So far, boss."

"Frank, what the hell are Russians doing in Nassau County? When I got my first look and smell of Oleg, the idea of drug dealing crossed my mind. Perhaps he betrayed the clan or branched out on his own. Sheba put the kibosh on that thought. We've stumbled upon a big-time bomb factory or warehouse. Drugs go the back burner, terrorism is now front and center."

"Well," Frank said, "at least we're not floundering around. Oleg's dead, and Grigori is the prime suspect. I say get the rope, arrest Glinka, and defuse the explosives."

"Easier said than done, Frank. Your prime suspect has been living in the shadows for six years. He's probably carrying false identification and passport. Guys like Grigori don't go down easy."

"Yeah, boss. But he botched the murder by leaving his name on the Glock's magazine ammo. That's amateur stuff. Grigori's blunder will lead to his downfall. A guy who makes that kind of goof will do it again."

"You're right, Frank. Put this case into the Police Academy lesson plan on Trace Evidence. The bad guy leaves something of himself behind and takes something with him. And that something with him is the murder weapon. Catch up with Glinka and the Glock, and it's case closed," I said.

"We'll start working on it right away, boss."

"Frank, it's time to order out the command post's bus. We'll be working out this scene for a while."

CHAPTER FORTY
COMMAND POST

Command Post buses are nothing more than boiler rooms on wheels, cramped with cubicles, chairs, and overworked sweaty bodies. Watching the driver back the bus alongside a pair of junk autos, I shuddered at the thought of how long I would call the CP my home.

"What a contrast," I said to Frank DiGregorio. "Only a genius like Picasso would have the ability to paint a mural of this scene."

"How so?"

"Frank, look over the pristine orange, blue, and white bus plastered with the police logo of a rampant lion in all his glory. Compare it to the dismal surroundings, a rundown decrepit building and grounds marked with junk cars, oil-soaked property, a morgue van, and a dead body. Quite surreal, don't you think?"

"You need to lighten up, boss," Frank said climbing onto the bus.

I followed and looked over familiar territory—computers, whiteboards, pull-down maps of Nassau County and other jurisdictions, faux-leather chairs posted in front of computer screens and keyboards, radio equipment, and a forty-inch flat-screen TV.

"Lieutenant, I'll leave the bus running awhile with the AC cranked up to hold down the temperature before your crew fills the place," the driver said.

"Thanks, Officer. I've been in this joint on hot days. The work is hard enough without having to sweat. Keep the BTUs turned up. I want to have a meeting."

The driver hit the AC controls allowing cold air to tumble from ceiling vents.

"Frank, assemble the troops. We have much to do."

Frank left the cool bus to round up the homicide team.

Expectant faces stared at me. Veterans of the drill, they knew what was coming.

"Is it time for the famous boss to-do-list?" Cassidy asked.

"Kevin, you're an irreverent bastard. If it wasn't for your skill sets, I'd get rid of you in a heartbeat."

A round of good-natured laughter broke the tension. I took the moment to go for my to-do list.

"I want you, guys, to work in teams. Bob Kowalsky owns the case. Ron Horton is his wingman. Kevin Cassidy and Taylor Morgan make up team two. Cassidy's the honcho, and Taylor is wingman . . . er, wingwoman."

Professionals, they had pen and paper at the ready.

"Team two drew the research straw. I want to know everything about this garage, down to who poured the concrete slab. Give me ownership, rent, taxes, electric bills, debts, arrears, and anything else to give us a direction."

Taylor wrote and nodded.

"That's not all. Dig up everything on Grigori Glinka. The fellow has to be somewhere, and not too long ago, he lived among us. Hopefully, he's still around to make another blunder. Trace him back to the Ural Mountains if you have to. I want to know what he eats, drinks, drives, and smells like. Get on it."

With that, Cassidy and Morgan booted up their computers and settled in for a long day. Placing check marks on my list, I turned my eyes to Kowalsky and Horton.

"You two are going on the road to root out Karen Arkady in Fair Lawn, New Jersey. The town isn't far from the George Washington

Bridge. Don't let her know you're coming. If she's not home, get moving to the orchestra. Find her and dig up everything useful on Oleg. Then go to his job and fill in the blanks."

Both men gathered their gear for the road trip.

"I'll plug her address into my telephone navigator," Kowalsky said.

"Keep in touch with Sergeant DiGregorio. Let him know if you need help. He's authorized to kidnap two cold-case detectives. Don't be shy. Use them if you have the need."

"Understood, boss," Kowalsky said.

I watched as they pulled away for the journey to the Garden State.

CHAPTER FORTY-ONE

MEDIA

"Frank, it's time to talk to the media. Watch my back and get me out if they become belligerent or redundant."

Gathering the media, print, and television news under the CP's windshield, I spoke in short declarative sentences. The usual suspects were spread in a semicircle: CBS, FOX News, Cablevision, PIX11, and print reporters assigned by *Newsday* and the *New York Post*. Finishing with the brief details, questions were hurled at me.

"What's the victim's name? What's the motive? What's the cause of death? What's the story on this garage?" they shouted.

Sticking to my script, I said, "We're withholding the victim's name until next of kin are notified. I don't want either a relative or friend to find out from the news that someone near and dear has been murdered."

"Fox News. Laura Lenihan here. How did he die?"

"The person is a victim of violence and, for the record, I didn't reveal the gender."

"*Newsday*, Shelby Lynde. Lieutenant, what's with this location?"

"Glad you asked, Shelby. That's being investigated as we speak. I have a team on it."

Lenihan raised her arm and shoved a microphone into my face. In a sarcastic swipe, she said, "You never tell us anything. Our viewers have a right to know what's the story."

"Laura, your viewers will know in good time. I won't reveal anything to impede the investigation at this early stage."

Frank came to the rescue. "Lieutenant McAvoy, the body is about to be transported. Please ask the press to make room near the morgue van. They may take photos from that angle."

"Thanks, Frank. Everyone move out to the road and make way for the body."

Like hungry children at a birthday party, the press corps took off, with their bags of cameras and notepads to snap photos of a shrouded corpse rolling into a black van. I was off the hook for now.

"What's next, boss?" Frank asked.

"The FBI."

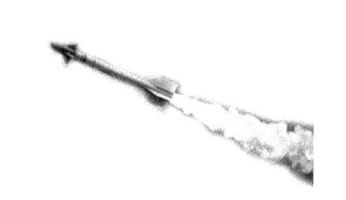

CHAPTER FORTY-TWO

Joint Terrorism Task Force

"Special Agent Finbar Scanlon, JTTF, may I help you?" a familiar voice asked.

"Fin, it's Patti Mac. I'm in the middle of a murder case. Before I get into it, I learned you had left the behavioral science unit in Quantico for the nightlife of New York City. What led to such a quantum leap?"

"Ahh, Patti. You never beat around the bushes. Your direct question deserves an answer. As you know, I joined the bureau after a stint in the Nassau County Police. The feds liked my street experience and put me to work on profiling serial killers. The work was exciting, the travel extensive, but I found myself bogged down in reading police reports. After a while, the luster wore off."

"Sounds like a career change, Fin."

"True, Patti. Some agents find Quantico is a safe haven. Most are married with children in good schools, happy spouses, and nice homes in the rolling hills of northern Virginia. They fell into a groove of Monday through Friday, weekends and holidays off. I don't carry the baggage, so I decided to return to my roots at Twenty-six Federal Plaza and take down the bad guys."

"I'm glad you're home, Fin. I need some advice. No, make that guidance. Russian national Oleg Petrovsky has been found in a shallow grave in Westbury with two bullets in his head. I have a sense of foreboding about the case."

"I'm all ears, Patti. Give me a sec to get some paper."

I heard him opening a drawer and a paper pad hitting the top of a desk.

"Go ahead, Patti. You've got the microphone," Fin said.

Before I could look at my watch, fifteen minutes had passed as I rattled off a summary, saving the best for last.

"At first, we suspected drugs, but our bomb-sniffing dog buried that theory in a hurry. We found a secret room being used as some kind of bomb factory. Nothing of consequence found except for a few flakes of trace evidence that might be C-4. As good as my squad is, I feel we may need some help with what may be some form of international terrorism. What do you think of that, JTTF man?"

"Stand by, Patti. I'm putting my supervisor on the line. She needs to hear this. Sorry, but you'll have to repeat the story. I'm with you. This sounds bad."

A short pause followed.

"Hello, Patti. This is supervisory special agent Kelly Anne Twomey," a pleasant voice announced in a lilting Irish brogue. "I've cleared my schedule for your story. Give it to me warts and all. Please call me Kelly."

By this time, I had the story down pat and recited my tale of woe. "We got lucky with Glinka's prints. Sometimes, the gods throw us a bone."

Twomey breathed into the phone, then said, "Do you want company? We can be at your scene in an hour. We can talk from my car."

"Sure thing, Kelly. I hoped you would join the battle. We could use your assets. Look forward to meeting you. Need directions?"

"No, Patti. GPS will park us at your front door."

Scanlon called me from Brooklyn's Belt Parkway as his crew left Manhattan by way of the Battery Tunnel.

"Fin," I said, "give me a summary of the JTTF so I don't look the fool in front of your supervisor."

"Well, Patti, it's an interesting story. Back in the day—J. Edgar Hoover's day—local law enforcement was considered the dregs. Truth be known, your department was at war with the FBI in the seventies. Seems a high-ranking chief was cheated out of credit for a kidnapping arrest that had taken place years ago. The chief never forgave the bureau and turned his boys loose to play havoc with the local bureau field office, especially on bank robberies. It was like a circular firing squad. No communication, no sharing of intelligence, and no cooperation. That was a snapshot of many FBI and local relationships."

"What turned it around, Fin?"

"Bank robberies in numbers that made the national debt look like piggy-bank change. The NYPD led the way in 1979, using the concept of combining federal and local skills. They married teams of local detectives and agents to work together and break down the walls. It worked so well, it was expanded to the counterterrorism program."

"What's the size of the program, Fin?"

"It started with eleven guys in New York City. Today's roll call lists a hundred and four JTTFs with four thousand troops. It's big, and you did the right thing to call us. Part of our mission is to investigate domestic terrorists operating the New York Metropolitan area."

"Thanks for the update, Fin. What a story. See you soon."

I felt a huge hand, the size of a baseball mitt, on my shoulder. "Boss," Frank said, "you should call your boss before loose lips give you up for calling in the Feds."

"Agreed, Frank. I'll do it right now."

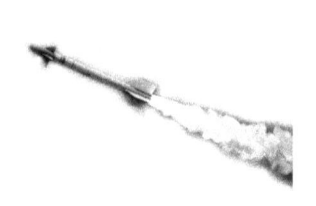

CHAPTER FORTY-THREE

Antagonism Meets Defiance

Before grabbing the command-post telephone, I checked the detective division on-call duty roster. I gave a moan, causing Frank DiGregorio to ask, "Are you all right, boss?'

Frank scanned the roster, found the name, and moaned. "Of all the creatures on call, you had to catch this bastard. Chief Corcoran's waist size is larger than his IQ," he said.

I punched in the number, knowing no good could possibly come from the notification. But it had to be done.

"JTTF? What the hell possessed you to put a call out to those pirates?" Deputy chief of detectives Andy Corcoran said.

"Chief, this case is developing into something beyond a routine Nassau County murder investigation," I replied, determined to hold my ground. "We have uncovered evidence of Russian participants in a murder and some kind of bomb factory in Westbury. It appears the executioner, Grigori Glinka, stamped his fingerprints on two ejected cartridges from the murder weapon. The victim is a Russian national and lives in Brooklyn. His girlfriend, also Russian, resides in New

Jersey. We could use the help and assets of the FBI, not to mention their manpower and unlimited funds.

"FBI, my ass," Corcoran shouted into the phone. "Federal Bureau of Incompetence. You've got a suspect. What's his name? Glinka? Find the bastard, bring him in, get a confession, and put the case to bed. Screw the FBI. Wave them off, Lieutenant. You were out of line to involve those bastards in our case. They'll steal your leads, lock up Glinka, take the credit, and you'll never hear from them again."

"I don't see it that way, Chief. I'm a graduate of the FBI National Academy, and I have a good relationship with many agents. I've always found them to be stand-up people, ready to help anytime I called."

Silence on the other end.

Knowing about Corcoran's checkered past from my father, I said, "Are you speaking from experience? When did the Feds screw you? Why the animosity?"

"Look here, Lieutenant," he said. "I don't give explanations to subordinates. You have your orders. Finish the job with Nassau County detectives. There is to be no FBI sniffing around in our business. Understand, Lieutenant McAvoy?"

"Understood, Chief. I'm too old a soldier to disobey a direct order."

I threw a hand grenade into Corcoran's ear.

"For the record, I intend to appeal your order to Police Commissioner O'Driscoll," I said emphasizing the word *appeal*.

"McAvoy, your dad is dead. You can't use him to get out of this. The PC will back my order, and don't ever threaten me again."

"Chief, since you brought up my father, I'd like to share a story with you. He told me about a sergeant who tried to hook up with a prostitute in a Manhattan nightclub. She lured him outside for a paid round of oral sex. He never had the pleasure. Two thugs, white guys armed with switchblades, were waiting behind a dumpster. After robbing the country boy from Long Island, they found his gun and badge. For the crime of being a cop, they cleaned his clock and put him in the hospital. Naturally, the lost gun and badge had to be reported to Internal Affairs. From the get-go, my dad said the sergeant's story had no believability. The sergeant couldn't identify his assailants, lied about where he had spent the evening, and claimed he was mugged by two black men."

Silence on the other end.

Corcoran's voice softened, and he said, "So, what's that got to do with me? You're throwing sand into the ocean."

"Perhaps. Perhaps not. I will suggest the PC open the IAU file on the sergeant. It will reveal the FBI was working an interstate organized crime case out of the nightclub. One of the muggers, a low-level gofer for the mob, was arrested and turned informant for the bureau. He surrendered up the sergeant's gun and badge, which was turned over to my father. The FBI buried the informant into the witness protection program and wouldn't produce him for an interview."

Dead silence on the other end.

"When called in to IAU, the sergeant saw his gun and badge laid out on my dad's desk and urinated in his pants. Because of the circumstances, the case was stamped inconclusive and the lying sergeant was not fired. Instead, he rose through the ranks. Last I heard, he made deputy chief of detectives."

Silence, broken with heavy breathing.

I am a predator. Predators go for the throat to kill prey. I went for Corcoran's Adam's apple.

"Chief, this case is going to be an involved, complicated investigation. I'm not a proud commander. I'll take help from Attila the Hun to solve the murder. The FBI is my enabler, a means to the end. I have no problem using them and giving back a little something from me. I live in a quid-pro-quo world. Scratch my back, and I'll scratch yours. I'm going to sign off now and call the PC for an appointment."

Silent as bullet-riddled Oleg Petrovsky.

"All right, Lieutenant," Corcoran said. "You presented a good argument. On second thought, use your friends from the FBI. I don't care. Just keep me in the loop."

Returning the phone to its cradle, I said to Frank, "That's a weasel my dad should have locked up. The Corcorans of this world are cockroaches, and they never change."

CHAPTER FORTY-FOUR

KAREN

I never put a call out to detectives to get an update on their progress. They check in to pass on something of importance. My call identifier showed Ron Horton's cell-phone number.

"Checking in from New Jersey, boss." he said. "We drove up on Karen as she was about to leave for her Manhattan concert hall, scheduled to perform in Beethoven's Ninth Symphony, the *Ode to Joy*. Our visit didn't bring her any joy. At first, Karen was hostile and defensive of Oleg. Totally uncooperative and told us 'I have nothing to say about Oleg'. That's when the diplomat, Kowalsky, told her we're homicide detectives. She clutched her chest and gasped, 'Homicide? What happened to Oleg'? After showing Oleg's pinky ring with her initials etched inside, Bob told her Oleg was the victim of violence, found murdered in Westbury, Long Island. Bob held out on how Oleg met his fate assuming she might say something incriminating about gunshots. She didn't."

"That's a good ploy. Many times, guilty people blurt out something only the police and the murderer know," I said.

"Correct, boss. Now, I'm no stranger to death notifications, but this woman took it hard. She fell to her knees wailing in primeval Russian, pounding her hands on the floor, screaming, Oleg, Oleg. Karen's crying was loud enough to cause the neighbors to call 911. They did, and I had to identify myself while Bob put on the 'Dutch uncle' act, got tissues for her face, and calmed her down. Since then, she's been a little more cooperative. Had a lot of questions for which we had few answers."

"What's her story, Ron?"

"To start with, her real first name is Ekaterina. She Americanized it to Karen. Claims it was easier to navigate through our culture with a recognizable name. Marriage to Oleg was penciled in to her calendar for next year. So far, she comes across as a legitimate person who emigrated in 2005 from Volgograd. She's a graduate of a musical university. Claims it's the equivalent of our Julliard School. Karen is good-looking, tall, blond, thirty-six years old."

"Tell me about Oleg. What's his story, Ron?"

"Ah, she got murky and defensive when I touched that nerve. Claims to know very little about his occupation other than he worked in some kind of 'security'. She gave his address in Brooklyn, an apartment in Brighton Beach, also known as Little Odessa. According to Karen, Oleg has a collection of strange-looking friends."

"Define *strange* for me, Ron."

"Karen described them as cheap gangsters, straight out of a 1930s James Cagney movie. Told us in no uncertain terms, if we go to Brooklyn we should bring Russian-speaking cops with us. Oleg's pals will clam up, and the best we'll get is *nyet*."

"What else, Ron?"

"Like her, Oleg landed here in 2005 and has some connection with the Russian government. Talked a lot about his days in Chechnya fighting the rebels when he had a few vodkas in him."

"Chechnya?" I said. "Isn't that close to where the Boston Marathon bombers came from? As I was told when I arrived in Homicide South, 'there are no coincidences in murder investigations.' Dig into the Chechnya angle for me."

"I'm ahead of you, boss. We're going to take a roundabout ride to the morgue for a visual identification of Oleg. I'll ride in the backseat with Karen and get all I can out of her."

"If anyone can, you can, Ron."

"Well, as I've always said, interviews and interrogations are a seduction. I have to convince Karen to tell me everything and make it look like it was her idea. It's obvious to us, Karen knows a lot more about Oleg than 'he's got strange friends.' By the time we travel from Fair Lawn to East Meadow, I'll have something more substantial. Hold on, boss. Kowalsky has some news. Be right back to you."

"OK, Ron. I'll wait. It's what I do best," I said into a dead phone.

Several minutes passed before Horton returned to the phone. "Boss, Karen lent Oleg her car, a 2010 blue BMW, New Jersey plates NFJ 312. He's had the car since April 15. Told Karen he was going to visit a friend."

"Name?"

"Oleg only referred to him as the 'general,' and they served together in Chechnya. She doesn't know what area Oleg was visiting. Karen has lent the Beemer many times to Oleg. It's not unusual for him to go missing for days, even weeks. That's why she didn't report the car missing in action," Ron said.

"So far, so good, Ron. Do your seduction in the back seat. In the meantime, I'll put out an APB on the Beemer. We've had one break so far. Maybe finding the car will give us another. Make me proud, Ron."

"Always, boss."

CHAPTER FORTY-FIVE

FBI Supervisor Kelly Twomey

I caught a glimpse of Kelly Twomey as she pulled into the crime-scene parking lot. Her government car, a navy-blue Crown Victoria was driven by my friend Finbar Scanlon.

"She's an Irish poster girl," I said to Frank DiGregorio. "Kelly looks like Maureen O'Hara with black hair."

He poked his head over my shoulder to get a look out the window. "Stunning. Old J. Edgar might have gone straight if he had agents like Twomey around him."

I laughed. "Frank, who the hell is holding all the juice to buy Crown Vics? Lotta dollars being dished out for those cars at every level of government. Every agency has a fleet of the damn things. Don't blaspheme J. Edgar around these people. He's still revered as an icon. C'mon, let's meet our allies."

Frank and I met the couple halfway. Four more allies arrived in a black Crown Vic.

"Light day at the office," I said to Kelly as we shook hands. Finbar and I hugged, borne of years of friendship. After all, we grew up together, went to the same high school, and landed in the same profession. We have a lot in common. "Fin," I said, "you haven't aged a day. Do you still get proofed at a bar?"

Kelly rolled her eyes. "Don't inflate his ego," she said. "He barely passed his annual physical readiness test. Finbar stays out too late, carousing," she said with a friendly smile.

After the obligatory exchange of introductions to all hands in the other car. I learned two were FBI and the others were detectives belonging to the NYPD. I invited them into the murder scene.

Pointing to a large pool of blood, Kelly said, "Oleg met his death here. Head wounds always ooze a lot of blood."

Pointing to the vault's shattered door, I said, "Let's take a peek at the place you're interested in, the bomb factory."

Kelly waved her arm as command to the mini JTTF crew who hit the room carrying satchels of tools of their trade. Explosive trace evidence tools. They moved as fast as kids on the last day of school.

"Leave them be. They know what they're doing. Show me the grave," Kelly said.

As we stared into the empty pit, Kelly confided, "This thing cannonballed up the chain of command to the director's desk in Washington. Russian involvement triggered a score of encrypted e-mails. I've been asked—no, told—to closely monitor the case and you."

"That means you're riding shotgun with me, Kelly. Since you're being straight with me, I'll do likewise. My boss hates the FBI. His cover story is you'll steal the case, make an arrest, and take all the credit. Truth be known, he had a run-in with the bureau in his younger days and was exposed as a criminal night crawler. I've no use for him, but we have to play the cards we've been dealt," I said.

"We'll have to watch each other's backs. Women have made a lot of progress in law enforcement, but we're still a minority in a white male environment," Kelly said.

"Amen to that, Kelly. Fifteen years into this game leaves me wondering if it'll ever change."

"It's getting late," I said. "Have you had something to eat? There's a diner not far from here. Care for a break? Our teams are beating the bushes, and there's not much to do until they report."

"Lead the way, partner," Kelly said.

CHAPTER FORTY-SIX

GETTING TO KNOW YOU

"The worst crime spree in the history of the Nassau County Police Department happened here," I said.

"This place?" Kelly said, looking around at customers dining on early-bird specials. "Looks like all the other diners in New York and New Jersey. Safe, well-put together, and more choices on the menu than most five-star restaurants can claim."

"That's true, Kelly. But on Memorial Day weekend years ago, a gang of five thugs invaded the place and held nearly a hundred people captive while they robbed, raped, and shot two people. It was known as the Sea Crest Diner in those days. The name has been changed to the Old Westbury Diner in an attempt to erase the ugly past," I said.

"Did the gang get caught?"

"Yes, the next morning, they were ran down and captured on the streets of Brooklyn."

My walk down memory lane was interrupted by a waiter who deposited glasses of water on the table and took our orders of two Greek salads and diet sodas.

"So, Kelly, tell me about yourself. I see you wear an engagement ring. When's the big day. Who's your significant other, and what does he do?"

"That's a story in itself, Patti. I need to tell someone, and you seem like a good listener."

"Look, Kelly, I was just making small talk—you know, woman-to-woman stuff. I'm not prying into your private life. Forget I asked," I said as I sipped my glass of water.

"That's OK. I don't mind sharing with you. It's a story unlike anything you've ever heard," Kelly said.

"All right, Kelly. Unload on Patti Mac."

"Ryan Collins was the perfect match. My proverbial soul mate. He was the one from the moment we met in the lobby of Twenty-six Federal Plaza in November, two years ago."

"Is he an agent?"

"No, a marine corps officer who stopped in for an application to become an agent. He asked me for directions to personnel, and I took a shot, introduced myself, and escorted him. Ryan was in uniform, and he looked like an artist's recruitment poster, not a human being. We chatted. He was temporarily assigned to the Brooklyn Navy Yard awaiting orders for deployment. I told him I would wait to answer any questions he may have after he picked up the paperwork. I fell in love when he said, 'Nothing I would like better, Kelly.'"

"Wow, you two were hit by Cupid's arrows."

"Yeah. Well, he invited me to be his date for the Marine Corps Birthday Ball to be celebrated the next week, on November tenth. Scarlet and gold are the marines' colors, so I found a gown to match. I felt like a Cinderella who had found Prince Charming. Tall, dark, and handsome with the hard, muscular body one would expect of a marine officer. Ryan tilts his head to the right when he laughs, and he laughed a lot that night. We began dating after the ball. When my birthday rolled around in January, he popped the question and slipped the bauble on my left ring finger. My joy was demolished when he revealed he had received orders for Afghanistan as an infantry platoon commander. I said yes to the proposal and cried because I was losing him as fast as I had found him."

Afraid to ask, but knowing I had to, I said, "Did he make it home, Kelly?"

"Yeah. Ryan was wounded twice and received the Navy Cross for saving his platoon from a Taliban trap. His deployment was extended while he recuperated, and he came home this year on April first. I met him at JFK's Terminal One. He was wearing captain's bars saddled with more medals than a third-world dictator."

"So, what happened, Kelly?"

"I wasn't the only person waiting in the terminal. Instead of heading toward me, Ryan pivoted and hugged his other visitor, a man."

I groaned. The image of Kelly's man dumping her for a guy was something I had not expected to hear.

"Who is the guy?" I asked.

"Not just any guy, Patti. The man was also dressed in a uniform. A black robe with the sign of the Jesuit order of priests sewn above his heart. Ryan and I stared into each other's eyes. Not a word was said. It wasn't necessary."

"So Ryan found God in a foxhole?" I said.

"Something like that, Patti. His platoon was under intense fire, surrounded, and about to be wiped out when Ryan prayed to God to save his men. Suddenly, a helicopter gunship showed up and destroyed the Taliban fighters. Intense pressure had made Ryan forget he's the one who called in the air strike on his own position, but he convinced himself God sent the helicopter. Still does."

"Sounds kind of biblical, like St. Paul on the road to Damascus and getting hit by a bolt of lightning."

"Good analogy. You and I make a living reading body language. The scene in the terminal told me Captain Collins had decided to become Father Collins. I know I can compete for his love against any other woman, or man, for that matter. But I can't compete with God. I don't have the juice for that combat. I lost my man, the only man I will ever love. Loss of love changes everything. Nothing in my life will ever be the same. I had my life with him planned out. I even chose a Chinese lullaby for our baby. It's called *Suo Gan*. I was fond of a line, 'Sleep my baby on my bosom'. That's never going to happen. I've lost my belief in a loving God and haven't been near a church since April first."

I winced at the thought of Kelly living without a child. It was a brutal reminder of my own condition. "Why do you still wear his engagement ring?" I asked.

"Good question, Homicide Commander. You are more than just a pretty face. Father Collins has embarked on a life of poverty, chastity, and obedience. I have chosen to remain celibate for the rest of my life also. I cannot, and will not, have sexual intercourse with another man. I display the ring to guys who hit on me to show I'm taken. Most walk away, and I leave it at that."

"Kelly, I thought I had a sad tale to share with you. My guy latched on to another woman and had a baby. My troubles are insignificant compared with your story."

Trying to find some other words, the silence was broken by a chirp from my cell phone. It was a text message from Taylor Morgan. *Have much info on auto-repair shop and Finbar has news from Moscow.*

CHAPTER FORTY-SEVEN
TRACKING GRIGORI GLINKA

Kelly and I gobbled down our salads and returned to the command post. I picked up the tab, and she left the tip. We were now partners looking out for one another. As we stepped into the CP, our eyes met two whiteboards filled with information. Finbar stood at the ready alongside his presentation.

"What do you want first, boss? The meat and potatoes on this repair shop or Moscow?" Detective Taylor Morgan said.

"First the station, Taylor. Fin, I assume you'll brief us on what the Russians have been up to."

Finbar said, "Oh, yeah. Taylor's briefing will take us directly inside the Kremlin."

Taylor pointed to her whiteboard and rattled off a detailed report. "I ran a UCC inspection through the New York secretary of state. There are no tax liens or debtors on file. The station is owned by the Bagration Corporation. At first blush, it's a front for a shell corporation. We'll be burrowing down into the weeds of corporation wheeling and dealing to get to the bottom of this one. But as you've been saying since this morning, boss. God is smiling down on us today."

My peripheral vision picked up Kelly's face. She didn't move or blink an eye at the mention of a kindly God.

"What made God smile?"

"I found out our department has a UCC image retrieval system account. It costs the job three hundred dollars a month. I pulled up the name of the lease holder, and it belongs to our shooter, Grigori Glinka."

Taylor paused for follow-up questions.

Kelly said, "Address, Taylor?"

"Yes. He used a Bronx apartment on Gun Hill Road as his home address. A directory search shows the place is real. I suspect he uses it as a dead letter box. We'll know more when we hit the place."

I chimed in. "Agreed, Taylor. Appropriate address for this case. What else?"

"Grigori doesn't have a car registered in his name. DMV shows a green Range Rover, New York plate GPZ 8807 registered to the address in the name of the Bagration Corporation."

"Good work, Taylor. I want you and Kevin to hotfoot it over to Josh Hirsch's office and use your feminine wiles to conjure up a search warrant for Grigori's pad. I hope we find more than a case of Stolichnaya vodka. Don't forget to include the bomb-sniffing dog's discovery and to ask for no-knock and nighttime endorsements. Obtaining a search warrant is time-consuming. We won't get to Gun Hill Road until later tonight. I'll call Josh Hirsch and let him know you guys are coming. In the meantime, I'll call for backup from our Bureau of Special Operations. I don't go anywhere without those guys. There hasn't been a time when I needed good police work that they didn't step up to the plate and hit a home run. I want them to eyeball the location and report back to you. It's important to describe the location for the affidavit. They'll probably reach out to you and Kevin with the details. And don't call the local NYPD precinct until we get near the location. I'll visit with the desk officer and clear the way for uniform backup."

Kelly's bomb technicians returned to the CP with their satchels full of samples and scrapings.

"Definitely explosive material in the room. The dog did a good job, and we're telling you there was a load of high explosives in the room. All gone now, of course," Special Agent Priolo said.

Kelly turned to Finbar. "Time for your dog-and-pony show, Fin. I hope it was worth making me miss dessert."

"To put it simply, Kelly. This is the *piece de resistance.*"

CHAPTER FORTY-EIGHT

Russian Security Service (FSB)

Special Agent Finbar Scanlon took the floor, smoothing a wrinkle from his suit while pointing a red laser beam at his whiteboard.

"Taylor and Kevin," he said. "hang out for this. There's a ton of information to add to your search-warrant affidavit."

I nodded and motioned for my detectives to sit and listen.

"I reached out to a deep contact in the American embassy in Moscow. We only use her for big-ticket items. I don't know about today's exchange rate, but we spent a bag of rubles for the information. Our lady in Moscow came through. First and foremost, Grigori Glinka is a lieutenant in the Federal Security Service known as the FSB. He's a graduate of the elite Federal Security Service Academy, graduating at the top of his class with the equivalent of our four-point grade. He's a comer and is only used for the most sensitive and highly classified missions."

"So," I said, "what's behind Glinka committing murder on American soil?"

"I'm coming to that, Patti," Fin said. "I want to report that the FSB is the successor to the KGB. Like their infamous daddy, the FSB is headquartered in Lubyanka Square, Moscow. It's named after a dismal prison in the square. For your information, the KGB's preferred execution method was a bullet to the head, like your man Oleg received."

"Fin, how large is the FSB," I asked.

"Big. It's a military service. Commissioned officers like Grigori don't wear uniforms. FSB has a uniform staff of sixty-six thousand including four thousand special-action troops. Border security comes under FSB jurisdiction and employs about two hundred and ten thousand guards. FSB is a combination of our ICE, NSA, Customs and Border Protection, Coast Guard, and the DEA."

"How did FSB get so powerful? What's their mission?" Kelly said.

"Destroying terrorism from Chechnya. The Chechens want to form a separate Muslim country. Since 2002, the Chechens have launched a massive terror campaign against Russian civilians, including the takeover of a Moscow theater. That was followed by a vicious attack on the Beslan grade school. Both sieges were put down by *Spetsnaz's* Alpha Group. *Spetsnaz* killed the terrorists, but many hostages also died."

"Sounds like an official policy of take no prisoners," I said.

"Correct, Patti. Russia's terrorist stats dropped from triple figures to double digits between 2005 and 2007. Our own Carnegie Endowment's foreign policy magazine named Russia as 'the worst place to be a terrorist'."

"Who's in charge of this monolithic organization?" Kelly said.

"Currently, the director is a colonel-general, a direct report to Vladimir Putin. At one time, Putin was in charge. Putin's resume includes time as a colonel in the KGB, serving in communist East Germany."

"Fin," I said, "I've known you for a long time. You always save the best for last. Give us your *piece de resistance*."

Finbar Scanlon reddened, smiled, and nodded.

"Oleg Petrovsky holds the rank of major in the FSB. He's been actively involved in the Chechen wars. According to my informant, Oleg was awarded the FSB medal for distinguished military service for actions in Chechnya during 2001 and 2002."

Silence.

Kelly rose, went to the whiteboard, then shook her agent's hand.

"Fin, Patti and I have a lot to chew on. Specialized Russian military personnel active on U.S. soil are harboring some type of bomb factory or storage facility. We now know Grigori, a junior officer, executed a decorated senior officer following the tradition of the KGB. An event like that has to be on the orders of senior officials."

Turning toward me, Kelly added, "What say you, Patti?"

"I'm glad I called out to the JTTF. We have neither the resources nor the assets to dig up information from the Kremlin. It's unbelievable. I need to think this through."

"While you're thinking, Patti, there's one more thing," Fin said.

"What?"

"Ten years ago, the FSB was given the legal authority to engage in targeted killings of suspects overseas, if so ordered by President Putin."

CHAPTER FORTY-NINE

END OF A LONG DAY

Half the streetlights were broken. No, change that to shattered by bullet holes. Target practice for the young guns. I caught enough light on my watch to read 10:30 p.m. It felt like two weeks since my day began in the Homicide Squad South office. The red telephone had taken me from Mineola to Westbury to the Bronx. As I pulled up to supervise the execution of the search warrant, I was struck by the dinginess of Gun Hill Road. A three-legged flea-ridden mutt and a Norway rat munched away at a garbage can buffet. Each had carved out his own seat at the table and deferred to the other. *I'll get mine and you get yours*—code of the street understood by the scavengers.

Gun Hill was a road of brick-and-mortar tenements. Rusting fire escapes fell from fifth-floor apartments to street level. First-floor windows were protected by iron vertical bars reminiscent of a prison cell. "Run and Gun" is the street term invented by the local cops.

"Prewar construction? I wonder how the tenants feel about living behind bars," Frank said.

"Would that be the War of 1812, Frank?"

"Better them than me, boss. I know a thing or two about places like this. Cockroaches and other crawly creatures thrive inside. Steel bars can't keep them out."

"Amen to that, Frank. Let's get to work. Tell Taylor and Kevin to round up the superintendent and bring him to my car. Deploy our plainclothes cops around the rear and side of the building in case our boy tries to pull a Houdini."

"Done, boss. They're on post, standing tall, as usual. Battering ram at the ready. I like Sergeant Connolly. He doesn't need detailed instructions. 'Been there, done that,' he told me."

I looked up and down the road and found Kelly and her JTTF team a block away, in reserve alongside a parked blue and white NYPD radio car in case we ran into trouble.

Taylor and Kevin marched the superintendent to my car. He wore the blank expression of a man about to be asked if he wanted a blindfold.

"Boss, meet Luis Munoz, the honcho of the hacienda. We found him in bed with a teenybopper. Luis claims the usual, *no habla ingles*," Kevin reported.

Weary of the world of bullshit, I said, "Put his large ass in the back seat."

Forty something, Munoz's belly testified to the fact that he ate and drank too much. He hung his head and stared at the floor mat.

"Look at me," I said, flashing my gold badge. "*Jefe*," I shouted to let him know who was boss.

Unaccustomed to dealing with a woman in authority, Munoz lifted his head. "*No habla ingles, Jefe*," he said.

"Give me his wallet, Kevin."

Poking through his documents, I found what I was looking for, a New York State driver's license.

I shoved the license in Munoz's face. "This means you speak English. Now start talking to me about apartment one-D or I'll empty the building and tell the tenants you did it. No *Feliz Navidad* tips for you this year."

Munoz nodded his head, a sign of surrender. "I speak a little English."

Whipping out an eight-by-ten mug shot, I said, "Luis, is this your tenant, Grigori Glinka?"

Peering at the snap, Luis' eyes darted about. "I don't know. I stay in the basement. Maybe it's him. I don't know."

Taylor Morgan ripped into Munoz in Spanish, a talent I didn't know she had. I picked up on words like *policia, jail,* and *Rikers Island*. Taylor shoved the photo into Luis's face. He sucked in a deep breath.

"OK. That's the man from one-D, what you call him, Grigori? That's not his name. Gregory is the name I hear," Luis said.

"How did you hear the name, Gregory? Was someone with him?" I said.

"Well, Mr. Gregory comes from time to time to pick up mail and packages. A few times, he had a woman with him. She called him Gregory. That's all I know. They were big tippers, and I stayed away from them."

"Does the woman have a name, Luis?"

"*Señor* Gregory called her Tanya. She's *muy caliente*."

"Explain, Luis," I said.

"It means very hot, *Jefe*," Luis said.

"When did you last see Grigori?" I said, disregarding his observation of Tanya's anatomy.

"Oh, he was here last week, around Thursday, I think. The lady Tanya was with him. She stayed in the car, combing her hair and putting on lipstick."

"What kind of car?"

"Oh, very expensive. A green Range Rover. Mr. Gregory gets parking tickets from time to time. I see him throw them in the backseat."

"Get your keys ready, Luis. I want you to open one-D for me," I said.

"I don't know. That would be breaking in."

"Do what I say, Luis, and you won't have any issues over the young girl in your bed."

"OK, OK, *Jefe*. I open up apartment one-D for you."

CHAPTER FIFTY

APARTMENT 1-D

Luis walked down the hall like a death-row prisoner at New York's Sing Sing prison: shuffling, head down, sweating, and shackled with keys instead of chains. Standing in the doorway of 1-D, he dropped his ring of master keys.

I said close to his ear, "If you're trying to warn someone inside, the first bullets will come through the door and put your lights out, Luis. *Comprende?*"

"*Si, Jefe.* I understand," Luis said.

Luis made a feeble attempt to insert the key into the door lock. His hands were trembling. I have no patience with malingerers and slackers.

"Did you suddenly get Parkinson's disease?" I said. "Put the damn key in the slot and get out of my way."

He did, and I shoved him aside. In we went, guns drawn, yelling and screaming like banshees. I was relieved to find the one-bedroom apartment empty. Neither Grigori nor Tanya were in the place. A quick scan showed the utilitarian furniture wasn't picked out by an interior decorator. I saw no television, no mail, no magazines, no phone, and no brochures. Waste disposal was empty. Opening the refrigerator, I found only a bottle of vodka, and the freezer held ice-cube trays. Closets and cabinet shelves were empty except for several plastic drinking cups. A dust-covered chocolate brown kitchen nook surrounded by two benches gave mute testimony that it hadn't hosted a dinner since it was purchased. Grigori's bedroom, laid out in military neatness, hadn't been slept in. Sheets and blankets were stretched tight. The window shade was drawn.

"This is a bust, Kevin. You and Taylor take the bed apart. Search between the mattress and box spring. Maybe Putin keeps his offshore rubles stashed there."

Kevin laughed. "Boss, Putin needs the whole building to stash his money. It's rumored his oligarchs pay tribute to him. Two for me, one for Putin."

"Get to it, you irreverent bastard. Watch out for creepy crawlies. I don't want them turning your pants cuffs into a new apartment and taking a ride in my car."

I ducked into the hall to update Kelly who answered immediately.

"Nothing here. Grant's Tomb has more stuff in it than this place. Afraid all I've done is tip Grigori off that we're on to him. Hold on, Kelly. I'm being summoned. Call you back."

Returning to the bedroom, Kevin said, "Boss, check this out."

Kevin and Taylor had stripped the bed and upended the full-size mattress and box spring. Duct taped to the coils were two treasures. A .40 caliber Glock, magazine in place, and a brochure giving details on how to pack and ship a Grinch missile and launcher.

"I know all about Glocks. What the hell is a Grinch? The thing looks like a modern version of a World War Two bazooka. Get on it, Taylor, and give me a story about the Grinch, and I don't mean Dr. Seuss's grinch."

"I'm on it, boss," she said as she parked her bottom at the kitchen nook and turned on her iPad.

By this time, Frank had joined me in the bedroom, and Kelly was out in the hall at his request. I strolled back to the hall and held a conference. As usual, I couldn't hold back my delight at hitting a grand slam in the bottom of the ninth. I asked questions aloud to no one in particular. "Grigori, did you have the stupidity to leave us Oleg's murder weapon? Top graduate in your elite Russian academy class? How many rubles did the diploma cost you, imbecile?"

Frank interrupted my diatribe against Grigori Glinka. "We'll photo the gun and brochure in place. I'll pack the evidence carefully for the lab techs. When they unwrap the duct tape, I'm willing to bet a month's pay Grigori left his prints on the sticky inside."

"Good thought, Frank. Get to it."

Ducking out to the hall, I lit a smoke and called Kelly.

"The count of Monte Cristo didn't have our luck. We hit the mother lode. Probably recovered the murder weapon, a .40 caliber Glock. We also picked up instructions for packing and shipping a Grinch missile. Have either you or Fin ever heard of the thing?"

"Yeah. I know what it is. We're coming up, Patti. Grinch is a Russian rocket launcher, so advanced it could take down Air Force One. I'll meet you in the hall. I know I don't have the authority under your search warrant to enter the apartment. I need to see the Grinch booklet."

Kelly and Fin arrived at warp speed. I didn't come close to finishing my cigarette as Frank handed me the paperwork and a receipt for Grigori notifying him we seized his property.

"Do I have to sign this, Frank? I know the law requires it, but it'll tip off Grigori that he had unwanted visitors."

"Yes, boss. Why risk a legal battle in court? You and I know Luis will tell Grigori as fast as the words can leave his mouth."

"OK, Frank," I said, as I signed his receipt.

Passing the booklet to Kelly, I said, "It was printed from the Internet, half in Russian, half in English. I can't figure out the damn Russian alphabet."

"It's in Cyrillic, Patti. Named for a medieval monk named Saint Cyril, who created the letters and words. It's the translation that scares me. This is a handheld weapon of mass destruction, and I think it was stored in Oleg's mausoleum. The question for all of us is, why is it here? What's the target? I'm going to photograph it and send it up the food chain, OK?"

I judged the Grinch information would put Kelly on the promotion road up the same food chain. She and Fin were allies, so I nodded.

While Fin and Kelly snapped photos, my phone rang. It showed Kowalsky's number.

"Go ahead, Bob. I have good news for you. How did you make out with Karen?"

"Pretty good, boss. She identified Oleg. That was unpleasant. It always is. She added a few things we didn't know. On the day he borrowed her Beemer, he said he was heading for Long Beach. At first, she thought he meant Long Branch, New Jersey, but he corrected it to Long Island. She only knows he was supposed to meet up with someone called the general."

"Name? Address?"

"Uh, uh, boss. Oleg was like the Sphinx. Hardly ever said anything about his work. She did tell us he had an important position in the Russian Federal Security Service, son of the former KGB, she said. We're taking her home to Fair Lawn. What's the good news? I could use some."

"We may have found your murder weapon taped under the bed. More importantly, we found photos of the thing that sent Sheba's tail waving. It's a Russian missile launcher named the Grinch. Kelly and Fin are all over it. We're going to wrap up here and head back to the command post. Let's catch up around ten tomorrow morning. It's been one hell of a long day."

CHAPTER FIFTY-ONE

Follow-Up

My team of four detectives, one sergeant, and I had caught the devil of a case. It's not our debut in the world of criminal investigation, but I felt they deserved a pat on the back. We gathered in the command post. I treated the team to a catered breakfast of bagels with all the trimmings. My order was delivered as the crew arrived to work.

"Yesterday was a tough challenge and only the best detectives could have handled it. Everyone did well. Thank you. Now we have follow-up reports and paperwork. No groans, please. Let's hear from Taylor on the results of her research into the Grinch."

Taylor went toward the whiteboard, scribbled a few acronyms like MANPAD, and turned to face her team. I thought about how well she had grown into this job and was full of self-confidence.

Passing around color photos of a handheld rocket launcher, Taylor said, "The picture is a Russian made Igla Grinch portable defense system. Forget about the word *defense*. The Grinch is a baby surface-to-air missile, a SAM. The Vietnamese used SAMs to shoot down American aircraft."

"Like the one that put Senator McCain in the Hanoi Hilton?" I said.

"Not quite, boss. McCain's SAM resembled a World War Two German V-2 rocket, several stories high. Our little Grinch can do the same job. All a soldier needs to transport the thing is a Jeep."

"We call that progress, Taylor. Continue."

"Right. Grinch and its cousins, the Gimlet, Grouse, and Gremlin are put together in a Russian factory in the city of Korlov. Each is equipped with one highly explosive missile. Grinch missiles like to hunt at night."

"What gear do they pack for that kind of morbid work?" I said.

"Infrared and heat-seeking radar. Grinch can take down either a MIG jet or a commercial airbus. It was built for one-shot, one-kill. Russia donated a boatload of the damn things to Libya and Venezuela. Al Jazeera has reported the monsters have fallen into the hands of ISIS."

"Break time," I said and motioned to Sergeant DiGregorio to meet me in the parking lot. I lit a smoke. "Frank, we have to send this up the food chain. Do it for me while I hear the rest."

Frank read his notes to Deputy Chief Corcoran while I stepped into the command post.

Kowalsky took his turn at the whiteboard. "I've put together a collection of APBs, boss. Karen signed a stolen-car report last night at the Fair Lawn Police HQ. Ron and I worded the APB for white male, Grigori Glinka, aka Gregory operating a green Range Rover. We didn't play with fuzzy language. It says arrest for murder. Glinka should be considered armed and dangerous. May be in the company of a white female named Tanya.' Before we broadcast the APB, I wanted your OK, boss."

"Get it done, Bob. Word for word."

Command post phones have an ominous crackle when they ring.

"Boss," Frank said, "the commissioner is on the line."

Grabbing the phone, I held it so Frank could listen in. I said, "Lieutenant McAvoy here. How may I help you, sir?"

"I'm on a conference call with your boss, Chief Corcoran. We've digested your reports and want to commend you for an outstanding piece of police work. The chief and I agree you should share your discoveries with the JTTF. They're going to owe us for this. I understand Chief Corcoran gave you his full backing on calling in the JTTF. Well done all around. I'm proud of you. Keep us informed," he said while hanging up.

Frank offered an Abraham Lincoln quote. 'Success has many fathers, failure is an orphan'. Corcoran has attached his wagon to your star. Watch him."

I nodded. "With six sets of eyes and ten ears, Frank. Make sure Kelly's updated."

BOOK FIVE

Russia is a riddle wrapped in a mystery inside an enigma.

Winston Churchill

CHAPTER FIFTY-TWO

ROSCOE, NEW YORK

July 5

Two a.m. phone calls generally don't bring good news like, "Hey, you just won the lottery." I shook off the first ring, hit the lamp switch, noticed the return phone number was blocked. and lit a cigarette.

"Lieutenant McAvoy here," I said. "Who died?"

Laughter. "Kelly Twomey on this end, Patti. You must lead a good life. God has tossed you another bone."

"Make my day, Kelly. Grigori's been found? Where are you?"

"I'm in an FBI helicopter heading to Roscoe, New York. Grigori is the reason for my call. One of our local agents is on the ground feeding me updates as she gets them. Get out your notepad. This is quite a story."

Sucking down a nicotine hit, I said, "I'm ready, Kelly."

"A New York State trooper on patrol in Roscoe stopped at the local diner last night for dinner. A young bearded white man named George Hoffman met him at the door and blew the trooper away with a question."

"And what was the sixty-four-dollar question, Kelly?"

'May I have political asylum'? The trooper handled it like an event he comes across every day. Never lost his cool. Patted down Hoffman and secured him in the backseat of the patrol car. Called for backup and a supervisor, then interviewed the stranger."

"What does Mr. Hoffman have to tell us?"

"Lots of stuff. A saga actually. Hoffman's an American citizen, born and educated on Long Island, who became radicalized, traveled to Syria, and joined ISIS. While in terrorist boot camp, he signed an agreement to wage jihad in his homeland. Something happened to give him cold feet."

"Jesus, Kelly. Do I have to wheedle it out of you? What turned this Hoffman fellow around?"

"He claims to have been holed up in a log cabin not far from the diner since early spring, guarded around the clock by military types. Hoffman had no visitors except for a man and a woman."

"Grigori and Tanya?" I said.

"Correct. We e-mailed Glinka's ID photo to the agent. Hoffman identified the man as Grigori—that's the Russian version of 'Gregory.' We don't have a snap of Tanya, so he could only describe her features. Matches the description of the woman seen at the mail drop in the Bronx."

"What is Hoffman's mission? Is he acting alone? Who are the guards?" I asked.

"He's been on standby for his assignment from ISIS. Grigori and Tanya never told him what was in the cards. He got that information yesterday from an elderly white man who scared the shit out of him. The visitor drove to the cabin on a bicycle, dressed like a beach bum wearing a New York Mets baseball cap. According to Hoffman, the bicycle man appeared to be the head guy. The guards deferred to him like he was a Roman emperor."

"What's Hoffman's target?"

"Bike man sat Hoffman down and outlined his orders. The target is an incoming passenger aircraft due to land at LaGuardia Airport this coming Friday night."

"What? Shoot down a passenger jet with what? Did he say?"

"Hoffman claims the weapon is a Russian-made Grinch handheld missile, proceeds from a looting he participated in while stationed in Syria."

"The same missile in the booklet from the Bronx?"

"Oh yeah. The Grinch is similar to our Stinger missile. We've documented a robbery of several Grinches stolen from a temporary Russian airbase at Tabqa, Syria, in August 2014. Reports of the theft were leaked by ISIS and carried in all the Al Jazeera newspapers."

"What inspired Hoffman to go to the diner, Kelly?"

"After the visit and a grueling argument between Grigori and the bike man, Tanya came into the main room and got involved in the dispute. Out of nowhere, bike man threw a crash helmet at her head. Screaming, he said, 'They found Oleg's body on a Monday. By Tuesday, the cops broadcast an APB for Grigori, the Range Rover, and Oleg's girlfriend's car. I didn't realize American homicide cops are so clever'."

"What happened then?"

"According to Hoffman, Tanya asks about the APB and is told,' I'm an old soldier who practices the art of spying on the enemy. I nearly fell off my bike when I heard them rebroadcast the alarm. How did the little shit Grigori made so many mistakes? I hold you accountable, Tanya. Here's what I want you to do'."

Realizing she was under suspended sentence of death, Tanya said, 'Anything you say, general.'"

Kelly continued, "Hoffman now claims the general issued a set of orders: 'First, get rid of the Rover. Eliminate Oleg's girlfriend. Turn the Bronx superintendent into a ghost. I'll take care of Grigori. He's about to meet Oleg in the afterlife.' Tanya left to carry out her orders. Hoffman fretted and developed second thoughts about taking out an aircraft loaded with women and children. Security went light after the general's visit. Grigori and the women were taken to the woodshed, under armed guard. Hoffman heard a volley of shots, cracked a window, found the diner, and waited for a cop."

"How did he know a state trooper would show up?" I said

"You know the answer, Patti. Cops gravitate to diners, and the Roscoe Diner is the only facility open for several miles around. So the trooper punched the info up the chain of command to my desk. We're getting ready to swoop in on the cabin and neutralize the Grinch. Care to join us?"

"Of course. I'll get suited up and bum a ride from our police helicopter. While I'm getting ready, I want to tell you the thing sounds fishy to me. It's too good to be true. Hoffman is locked up under maximum security, then the guards disappear allowing a prime trained assassin to walk away. God doesn't throw around those kinds of bones. What else, Kelly?"

"Hoffman teamed up with another radicalized American assassin in Syria's ISIS boot camp. His name is Andrew O'Leary, whereabouts unknown. We're running a background check on him as we speak."

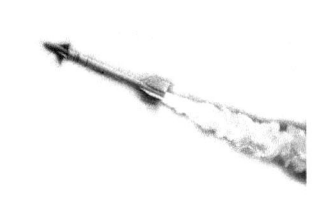

CHAPTER FIFTY-THREE

DOUBLE CROSS

This time, the caller didn't block her number.

"Hi, Kelly. Are you on the ground?" I said.

"Yeah. Just landed in the Roscoe Diner parking lot. Almost empty at this time of morning. My people and the state troopers are about to hit the cabin. Hoffman is with them, handcuffed inside a trooper's van. They needed him to point out the correct location."

Fearing Chief Corcoran's warning about FBI glory hunting might be coming true, I said, "Why the hurry, Kelly? Sounds like you've revved up the pace of the response to match the speed of the Indy Five Hundred."

"Good question, Patti. Since we spoke, Hoffman has revealed the young women recruited for the job are from Pakistan, trained to wear suicide vests for a bang-up show this Friday night. The stage is set for one to blow herself up at Citi Field during a baseball game. The other will attend a Manhattan synagogue Sabbath service and do the same. According to Hoffman, the vests are stored in a woodshed. His Grinch missile launcher is keeping the vests company. We had to move fast in case the guards found Hoffman MIA and disappeared with the explosives and the *shahida*."

"*Shahida*?"

"Translates to female martyr," Kelly said. "They don't use the word *suicide*. It's against the teachings in the Koran. Mass murder is acceptable, but not self-inflicted murder. Tough enemy we're up against."

My watch showed 3:30.

"*Tough* is an understatement. We'll have wheels down by five o'clock in the diner parking lot. Can you arrange for cars to take my team to the cabin?"

"Already done, Patti. I'll keep you updated. As soon as I know something, you'll know."

Kelly made me feel better about a future phone call to Chief Corcoran. At least I could counter his barrage of "I told you so's."

"Thanks, Kelly."

Frank DiGregorio, sitting on my right, said, "Time to call the duty officer. This case is turning into front-page headlines and has multinational roots. You'll have to tell the bosses, boss."

I nodded. Frank was right. I also knew I would catch hell for hijacking a police helicopter in the middle of the night. Their use is restricted and may only be authorized by a boss at the chief level, not a lowly squad commander named Lieutenant McAvoy.

"You're right as usual, Frank. I'll call it in when we land. The bastards may order me to turn the chopper around and return to Nassau County. By calling in later, I can report that I had nothing to say until I got to the scene."

"Boss," Frank said, "you're going to play that game once too often. Try to remember Corcoran and his kind have scores to settle with your old man. Big Mac is dead, so that leaves you to pay for the sins of the father. They can't wait to take you down. I recommend you call headquarters sooner than later."

I stared at Frank but had nothing to say. How does one argue with facts?

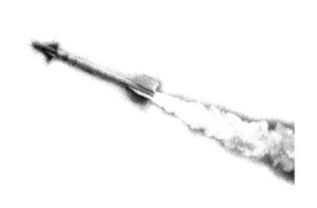

CHAPTER FIFTY-FOUR

Log Cabin

Kelly kept to her word. A pair of state-trooper cars carried my team to the cabin. I drove with Taylor while Bob Kowalksy and Frank DiGregorio followed. Ron Horton and Kevin Cassidy were on the way in another chopper. We turned into a private driveway nearly the length of a football field. We got out and joined our federal partners.

Kelly said, "The cabin is deserted. Lights out. No one home. Scope it out while I update you."

In we went, and the only word to describe the place was *palatial*. We passed through a wraparound porch. In place of beams stood carved bears supporting the roof. Adirondack chairs, arranged neatly like soldiers on parade, didn't have the appearance of ever being used. Wood fireplaces decorated the walls of many rooms. Carved mountain lions lay on each mantle, sprawled over the hearth.

"We're taking a peek into the woodshed. It's at the edge of the tree line, and it's the size of a two-car garage. Finbar is leading the crew," Kelly said.

"Don't you need a search warrant?"

"Ordinarily. Under the Patriot Act, we have the authority to conduct what amounts to a 'peek warrant.' If it's stocked with weapons of mass destruction, we'll have to send out for lunch. Then we'll be here all day and night. I intend to go slow," Kelly said.

"Good tactic, Kelly. We don't need to witness a post Fourth of July extravaganza with limbs of agents and troopers dangling from the trees. How is Fin managing the peek?"

"Careful as a man walking on thin ice. We know there are probably several bodies in the shed, but it could be booby-trapped. He's using similar equipment you used at the Westbury murder scene. You know, a minicamera attached to a movable snorkel. He's feeding it under the door to take a look around for contraband. I kind of hope the guards took the stuff with them after Hoffman absconded."

"I agree, Kelly. It would make no sense to leave valuable weapons of mass destruction behind. Hoffman's gang can easily change targets. Missiles, launchers, and explosives are hard to come by. Victims may be found anywhere. Everything is a soft target. Change Citi Field to a mall. Pencil in a concert hall for the synagogue. ISIS doesn't care who dies as long as the event is the lead story on CNN."

I lit a cigarette while Kelly answered her cell phone.

"Put that out," Kelly said. "Finbar has news. No sign of explosives, but he's examining three dead bodies, a man and two women, wrapped in black ISIS flags. His team is popping the door. Let's go."

I stomped on my cigarette after one puff, asking the team to follow me. Filling them in on the pathway to the shed, I said, "We have to show deference. This isn't our crime scene. We're here to observe and gather intelligence for our case. Understood?"

Everyone nodded.

My interest and eyeballs took in the features of the dead man. After comparing his face to Grigori's ID mug shot, I announced, "Oleg's case is closed. The murderer has been murdered. Looks like he took two shots to the back of his head."

Taylor and Bob examined the women's bodies. "Likewise, boss," Bob said. "Two bullets each in the back of the skull. No exit wounds, and there's a .40-caliber Glock in the corner. No attempt was made to conceal it. Everything is bizarre with flags wrapped around them. Wrapping had to be done postmortem. What does it all mean?"

I didn't have an immediate answer for Bob. Thinking for a while, I said, "Grigori was eliminated for a reason. A star pupil on the fast track to promotion doesn't get wasted on a lark. People like Grigori are mentored, trained, indoctrinated, nurtured, and brought along for bigger things than two bullets in the head. This is mass murder designed to get our attention on the crime and off some other sinister project. I'm convinced of it. I can't shake the feeling. The Roscoe murders are part of a devious three-act play."

CHAPTER FIFTY-FIVE

INTERROGATION - GEORGE HOFFMAN AKA YUSUF AL-MUSLIM

Our murders are examined by crime-scene units. The FBI employs an evidence response team. Same mission, different names. Kelly's ERT was poring over the woodshed taking more pictures than a wedding photographer.

Reduced to the role of a civilian bystander, I stood outside sucking on a Parliament Light 100. I blew the smoke into the air as I watched Kelly approach me.

"This is going to be a long day for you. The ERT will take the shed and cabin down to the floorboards. There's not much for you and your team to do, Patti," Kelly said.

Polite. But I knew it was a courteous suggestion to return to Nassau County, close out the Oleg Petrovsky case, and move on to the next victim. I didn't want to do it. Every fiber of my being told me to talk to Hoffman. The words stuck in my throat, but I found myself committing an unpardonable sin. Me, Lieutenant McAvoy, Homicide South Commander, had to ask for permission to debrief Hoffman, now a federal prisoner.

"Kelly, there is one thing to do before we leave," I said.

"I know. You want words with Hoffman. I can't do it officially, Patti. But if I go into the cabin to supervise the search for evidence, I can't watch Hoffman. You've got fifteen minutes. When I come out of the cabin, that's it. Get out of the car and go home. Agreed?"

"Thanks, Kelly. Fifteen minutes will have to do."

Pivoting, I caught Kevin Cassidy's eye and motioned him to my side.

"Back me up, Kevin. Hoffman's the target. I want to get everything out of him. We've got a short time."

I asked the trooper to take a coffee break, and I slid into the backseat alongside Hoffman. Kevin's hand draped over the steering wheel.

Before I introduced myself, Hoffman said, "I've been watching you puffing away on the nicotine sticks. Within minutes, I put a name with your face. I know who you are. You're Lieutenant McAvoy. I've seen you on television. What's a Nassau murder cop doing up here in the mountains?"

Direct. His eyes buried into mine. I went for it.

"I want to know all about you and Andrew O'Leary. Two Long Island college boys turned ISIS mujahedin."

Hoffman smiled. "You used the correct term. I respect your knowledge. I am a holy warrior. America is a violent country of infidels and can only be cured through violence."

"You avoided the question, George. What about you and O'Leary and conversions to Islam? When and where did it take place?"

"I'll speak for myself. Please refer to me by my nom de guerre—Yusuf Al-Muslim. My conversion began at university where I was dormed in a suite with five other students. Three were practicing Muslims, praying five times a day. In my freshman year, I paid little attention to them. Engineering is a difficult subject, and I had to knuckle down."

I decided to play along. Let him talk and lead me to O'Leary.

"Then what happened, Yusuf?"

"Over time, we remained suitemates. It became apparent that Islam is a religion of peace and equality. The boys in my suite practiced civility toward everyone, including female students. They translated their prayers into English for me, and I evolved into a believer of Islam."

"How long did it take?"

"By the end of my sophomore term, I began attending prayer services at mosques. I had a prayer rug for my room. My conversion was complete when I swore to adhere to the five pillars of Islam."

I have some knowledge of Islam. To keep Yusuf talking, I asked, "What are the five pillars?"

CHAPTER FIFTY-SIX

Five Pillars of Islam

Yusuf couldn't shut up, which is what I wanted.

"The first pillar of Islam is *Shahada*, the oath of every Muslim. 'I testify there is none worthy of worship except God and I testify that Muhammad is the messenger of God.' *Shahada* is our answer to the Christian baptism. Incidentally, Islam means 'submission to God.'"

"Powerful stuff, Yusuf," I said to feed his ego. "What's number two?"

"*Salah*, our obligation to pray five times a day."

"I understand *Salah*. I've seen many documentaries showing the faithful praying in mosques. Men and women are separated, aren't they?"

"Yes," he said. "It's a tradition. Let's talk about *Zakah*, pillar number three, which means 'charity.' We are required to help less fortunate Muslims. *Zakah* is similar to the Christian practice of tithing."

"Yusuf, I feel like you're taking me on a tour of Islam," I said.

"As you can see, Lieutenant. Islam is a peaceful religion. For example, *Sawm* is the fourth pillar, dedicated to fasting. We typically fast either for repentance or to commune with God. All of us fast during the holy month of Ramadan."

"And number five, Yusuf?"

"That's one pillar I haven't had the honor to achieve. It's called the *Hajj*. Once in every Muslim's life, he or she is required to make a pilgrimage to Mecca, if circumstances permit."

"I came across the *Hajj* in one of my cases in Long Beach several years ago. Why didn't you go to Mecca?"

"Time didn't permit me to make the trip. I hope to visit Mecca when this matter is cleared up and I will be free to move about."

I didn't want to rain on his parade, knowing he faced a lengthy prison term for his involvement with ISIS. Instead, I kept him talking.

"Is there anything else you would like to share in your conversion?"

"Yes. I subscribe to Sharia, a legal system and code of conduct covering criminal law, government, and other issues."

"Such as?"

"Marriage, punishment, inheritance, banking, worship, charity, and civil matters. We consider Sharia to be the only respectable law."

"I respect your conversion and commitment to Islam, Yusuf. You claim it's a peaceful religion, yet you prepare for undeclared war on innocent civilians. Mass murder and rampage are not listed in the five pillars, are they?"

"Clever tactic, Lieutenant. I told you. America is a violent country dropping hellfire missiles from unmanned drones all over the ISIS caliphate. America kills more Muslims in one day than all the so-called terrorist attacks put together. I am a believer in Islam, but for the moment, I am a holy warrior."

Shifting from Islam, I said, "Tell me about the change from holy warrior to becoming a handcuffed prisoner in the back of a police car. What prompted your conversion, Yusuf?"

"Good direct question, Lieutenant. It deserves an honest answer. After I was recruited and sent to ISIS camp in Syria, I filled out an application. I was asked if I wanted to become a martyr or go to war as a mujahideen. I checked off the mujahideen box and went through three months of physical and ideological training, partnered with Andrew O'Leary or Ahmed Yamin."

"His nom de guerre?"

CHAPTER FIFTY-SEVEN
ANDREW O'LEARY AKA AHMED YAMIN

"Yes. Ahmed and I became close friends and helped out with the break-in at a Russian air base in Tabqa. We stole a dozen Grinches and dozens of launchers to be used on the infidels. The building was protected by two sleeping security guards who were eliminated. Following the robbery, Ahmed and I went through extensive training and practice launching the missiles. He was a better student and was given the honor of taking down a Syrian helicopter. Ahmed shot the chopper down with one bull's-eye."

"Have you taken down an aircraft, Yusuf?"

"No. My training was on brick-and-mortar buildings. I was led to believe my military and Grinch skills were to be used destroying either government or corporate structures."

"What happened to Ahmed? Is he here?"

"Ahmed and I returned to the United States by separate routes. I have no idea where he is or what mission they gave him. I do know two Grinches came to America with us. One with a live missile was stored in Roscoe for my assignment."

"For the passenger jet at LaGuardia Airport?"

"Yes. The general on the bicycle was adamant about my orders. When he sensed hesitation on my part, he ranted and raved. Claimed 'I was told you volunteered for the job and couldn't wait to fire a Grinch at the target.' I told him I had signed on to engage in holy war and, if necessary, die in jihad, not in suicide at a New York airport. Suicide is forbidden by the Koran."

"What did the old man do?" I said.

"He stormed out of my room. He ripped into Grigori with an ass-chewing unlike anything I have ever heard. Grigori started to give as good as he got."

"How?"

"He blamed the mix-up on me. Grigori swore that I had thrown myself wholeheartedly into the plot from Tabqa to Roscoe. Then the old man told him something I didn't understand."

"Which was?"

"I should give you what Oleg got, right here on the floor of this log cabin. You aren't worth dirtying up the floor with your blood. The police have alarms out for you. What mistakes have you made, Grigori? The guards moved toward the men. Grigori saw them, fell to his knees, begged for mercy, and cried like a small boy who had embarrassed his father. The old man hustled the guards off to the side and mentioned Ahmed's name as a candidate for the LaGuardia job. That's when I knew I was in big trouble."

"What kind of trouble, Yusuf?"

"Assassination. Get rid of the coward and leave the job to a real holy warrior."

"Tell me about the guards and the general. Are the guards Muslim? Where are they from?"

"I think the guards are Muslims—at least they pretended to be Muslims. From the little they said, I got the impression they were from Central Asia. Specifically, from Russia's former republics of Kazakhstan or Azerbaijan, now independent Muslim countries. Like me, they prayed silently as they kept an eye on me. I think the praying was for show. Anyway, I made up my mind to turn myself in to the first cop I saw. I will not commit suicide or be murdered after taking down the LaGuardia plane. Does that answer your questions, Lieutenant McAvoy?"

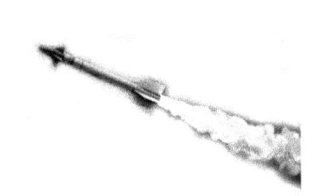

CHAPTER FIFTY-EIGHT
TRADECRAFT

Noticing my attention was diverted from my watch to the cabin door waiting for Kelly to pull her prisoner out of my backseat and end the interrogation, Cassidy took over.

"Yusuf, I'm going to go through your wallet," he said, reaching into Yusuf's back pocket.

Like his previous smiles, Yusuf grinned, almost smirked, at the request.

"Go ahead, Detective. You'll take it anyway."

Kevin rifled through the wallet, a rather thin leather pouch, with a few slots cut out for license and credit cards.

"You don't seem to carry much, Yusuf," Kevin said. "I don't see anything here other than a driver's license, a New York City subway MetroCard and a hundred bucks. That's traveling light."

"Detective, that's called tradecraft. ISIS trainers honed in on FBI and police tactics for building a criminal case against us. Your allies in the woodshed and log cabin call it searching for pocket litter. We were trained to avoid carrying anything to link us either to other fighters or a group of mujahideen. The driver's license in your hand shows my parents' address, which is designed to take you up a dead end. Weeks of indoctrination revealed the way to get caught and convicted is through link analysis. Your kind likes to rummage through our house and cell phones, laptops, friends, and family. Ahmed and I learned to faithfully follow the training protocols."

"And they were?" Kevin said.

"We leave neither paper nor electronic trails for the infidels to follow. We are like the night fog, dark, cloudy, with diminished visibility. As soon as the sun rises, we're gone without a trace."

I interrupted.

"Yusuf, if you thought the old man was about to dispatch you to paradise, how come your escape was so easy?"

Pondering his answer, Yusuf said, "I analyzed your question several times. Remember, Lieutenant, I am a trained engineer. Problem solving is my forte. I concluded the old man wanted me to leave and torpedo the mission. I began life in the log cabin as his perfect messenger of death who turned into a nightmare. I came to the conclusion Ahmed was about to be promoted as a missile launcher for a target unknown to me. Regardless of who pulls the trigger, I consider shooting down a planeload of innocent civilians as mass murder, something I never signed on for."

"Are you sure about Ahmed?"

"He excelled in training and earned his reputation with turning a Syrian helicopter into debris. He handled the Grinch the way some men handle a shotgun at a skeet shooting range. They don't aim at the target. The shotgun trigger is pulled to intercept the clay pigeon where it's going to be."

"Why would Ahmed and his handlers take a chance with the target now? We'll cover LaGuardia and the other targets with a thousand agents and cops. He'll be caught."

"Ahmed must have been given another target. Like the skeet shooters, sometimes they send up two pigeons. While you're aiming your weapons at LaGuardia, he'll be somewhere else. And remember this, Lieutenant McAvoy. Ahmed's ISIS application was identical to mine. He checked off the box marked martyrdom."

CHAPTER FIFTY-NINE

SKULLDUGGERY

Kelly ambled over to the state trooper's car. I stepped out to intercept her, leaving Cassidy a second shot at Yusuf, man-to-man stuff.

After lighting another cigarette and blowing the smoke into the morning air, I told Kelly every detail of the backseat interrogation. I didn't want to withhold any information from my federal friend. That, and telling the tale bought Cassidy a few more minutes.

Kelly was intensely interested in the location of Ahmed's weapons of mass destruction. She said, "Are you sure Yusuf is being truthful with you and Cassidy?"

"Kelly, there's one truism in the world of murder and suspects. Caught, trapped, snared or whatever, men like Yusuf always hold something back. I've asked Kevin to burrow into Yusuf's mind for a few more minutes."

"I'm afraid that's all the time I can spare," Kelly said. "Washington's all over this like a predator drone. The news media is getting a slanted story. Officially, a triple murder never happened in Roscoe, New York."

"How can you cover up three hits?" I said. "Too many people involved. Your team, my crew, and don't forget the state troopers. One loose tongue fueled by beer will blow your story."

"Just following orders, Patti."

"Christ, Kelly. The Nazis used that line at Nuremberg. It didn't work then, and it certainly won't work now. When the story is exposed, Kelly Twomey will be named the scapegoat. The cover-up is always worse than the crime, at least to the news media. Bet your retirement pension on that little bit of sage advice," I said.

"The press release is being typed as we speak," Kelly said.

"What, pray tell, did the FBI bureaucrats call a triple murder?"

"Officially, the release reports an old story of a classic adulterous affair gone bad. Husband and wife rent a log cabin for a weekend getaway. They're tracked by the husband's lover. After a terrible fight and the usual recriminations, guilt, and depression, husband takes the easy way out. He kills the women and turns the gun on himself. Grigori put two bullets in the back of his skull."

"C'mon Kelly, no one's going to buy that line of BS," I said.

"First of all, there is no Grigori. Aliases have been inserted into the press release. My people have been spinning BS since the birth of the bureau. Give them credit."

"What about the medical examiner and the autopsy? How can the bureau cover that up?"

"Three bodies are heading to Washington for postmortems. Fill in the blanks. Murder, suicide, case closed." Kelly said.

"Good luck, Kelly. I don't see the justification. Sounds like a James Bond bit of skullduggery. How are you going to get around the state troopers? The bodies belong to them and come under their jurisdiction." I said.

Kelly smiled, the kind of smile one makes when dealing with a child who doesn't grasp the subtlety of a situation.

"Superintendent DiTomasso, a former FBI assistant director, is in the loop. It's a question of national security, and those two words close a lot of file cabinets," Kelly said.

I grasped the meaning. Three murders never happened, Yusuf goes into the Witness Protection Program, and I wind up with a solved murder of Oleg Petrovsky. Somehow, I feel the report on the Petrovsky case will never be written. National security and all that nonsense. I needed another cigarette and was lighting up when Kevin approached.

"Boss, Yusuf doesn't have much more to add to the story except for this. During the argument and before he slipped out the window, he overheard two words."

"And?"

"*Long Beach.*"

"New York's Long Beach or Long Branch in New Jersey?"

"Yusuf says 'Long Beach'."

CHAPTER SIXTY
COVER-UP

July 6

Inside the Nassau County Police Department several code words are used to let the person on call know there is to be no discussion. One of them is "forthwith." The police commissioner's office is known as the 'front office.' A summons to the front office forthwith means put your Crown Victoria police car engine on afterburners and move out.

There she was, Miss Perky, an unarmed uniformed female police officer who acted as gatekeeper for the inner sanctum. She spoke like I was an errant student standing in the corner until the principal was ready for me.

"Wait here, Lieutenant. I'll see if the PC is available to see you. I don't see your name in the appointment diary," Perky said.

"You wait. I was given a forthwith summons, and even a paper shuffler like you should know what it means. I'm going in. Don't get in my way, young lady, or I'll have your ass walking a beat on the midnight tours," I said.

Perky backed off, not realizing my threat had as much substance as smoke from one of my cigarettes.

"Go right ahead, Lieutenant McAvoy. I won't stand in your way," Perky said.

Two heads sat in the front office. One belonged to Commissioner O'Driscoll and the other sat on the shoulders of my nemesis, deputy chief of detectives Andrew Corcoran. *No good can come from this*, I thought.

"Please sit, Lieutenant, Andy and I want to congratulate you and yours on a job well done. We've just reviewed a report from ballistics confirming the Glock you seized in the Bronx was the murder weapon used on Oleg Petrovsky. The murderer has been murdered.

"I spoke to the director of the FBI. His agency will assume jurisdiction under the cover of national security. There'll be no messy trial revealing international intrigues. It must give you a great deal of satisfaction to mark the case closed. Sort of like a football coach winning a play-off game and moving on to the next challenge."

"We still have many leads to follow, Commissioner. I don't see the case closed," I said.

Corcoran began to speak, and it was obvious he was primed by the PC.

Uh oh, here it comes.

"We don't see the need to waste valuable manpower on investigating a closed case. It's time to bury the investigation with Oleg. If any inquiries are made, refer them to Crime Stoppers at the usual number, one eight hundred TIPS. Understood, Lieutenant?"

"How should I conclude the report? Case closed by order of Deputy Chief Corcoran?"

"There won't be a formal report. Reports get leaked to the hungry media. That's not happening on my watch. And one more thing, Lieutenant. You will not arbitrarily use the police helicopter without a chief's permission. We can't have Homicide South running excursions up and down the east coast."

"Chief, what about the weapons of mass destruction?" I said.

"That's an FBI problem now. They wanted it. They got it. In hindsight, we're elated you called them in on the first day. Showed good instincts. Let the FBI run with it. They're equipped with manpower, assets, and money."

"Chief, there was mention of Long Beach during a fierce argument in the log cabin. May I at least liaison with the Long Beach Police Department. They're a first-rate bunch of cops, and I'd like to have them sniff around for us. Perhaps put some money on the street?"

"No," Corcoran said. "Put your friend Kelly in touch with the Long Beach cops. If there's any sniffing to be done or dollars to be paid, let the FBI pay for it. Lord knows they have a money tree blooming on the director's terrace."

O'Driscoll watched his chief and didn't like what he heard. Ever the patriarch, he said, "Give your team a couple of days off. They deserve it. A terrorist operation on American soil has been uncovered, and it's due to your heads-up thinking."

"Commissioner, but—" I interjected.

"No buts, Lieutenant. Homicide South is off the case. The decision's been made."

"Yes, sir," I said.

CHAPTER SIXTY-ONE

COINCIDENCE

July 7

"To hell with time off. The PC wants us to bury the case under a special category known as 'national security,'" I told my team as we assembled in the conference room.

Kowalsky, who owned the case said, "What should I say in my final report, boss?"

I didn't have the heart to tell him that as far as the world was concerned, he had no case. Kowalsky isn't the kind of detective who understands office politics. Everyone sat around waiting for some kind of direction from me, and I had little to say. We chatted. They knew something was wrong, and I didn't want to share the bad news with them.

At eleven o'clock, Ginger McCullough opened the conference-room door.

"Kelly Twomey is on the phone. Line six."

"Patti," she said, "put on CNN. Karen Arkady's been murdered in a subway station in New York City. A pocketbook snatch gone bad. The perp made a grab for her purse in the classic fashion. He cut the strap with a box cutter, but he didn't count on Karen's toughness. She resisted, kicked him in the groin, and he pulled out a handgun and popped two shots into her head. The bad guy is a white male, thirties, and nondescript. The whole thing was caught on the subway station CCTV. Goddamn city is going to hell."

I grabbed the remote and switched on the TV. CNN was replaying the scene for the world to watch the lawlessness of the Big Apple. Karen was seen falling onto the platform, dead before her head hit the tiles. It didn't take long for her head wounds to spill blood. She lay there while passengers stepped around her. The perp had run off in the other direction and was long gone. Horton and Kowalsky were mesmerized by the scene. After all, they had been the men who had spent time with her early on in the case. It was like watching the death of a friend.

Ginger was back, this time with a call from a Bronx homicide detective.

"Lieutenant, this is Detective Robinson. I'm at the scene of a murder of one Luis Munoz. The reason I'm calling you is we searched the body and found a receipt from a search warrant you executed in apartment one-D of his building."

"How did Luis meet his maker?" I said.

"Two gunshot wounds to the back of his skull. Found him in a basement apartment. We got an anonymous nine-one-one phone call. As of now, there are no witness, and no one knows anything. Is there anything you can do to help us out?"

Before I got into a discussion with a strange voice over the phone, I needed time to think this through.

"Give me your number, Robinson. I'll get back to you."

I called Kelly to give her an update.

"Tanya obeyed the general's orders," she said. "No chance of a coincidence?"

"Kelly, there are no coincidences in murder investigations. Two significant players are removed the same day by violence, one the same way as the log cabin murders and the murder of Oleg. Two shots to the back of the head. No, Kelly, the killings are connected and designed to get rid of potential loose ends."

After hanging up, I felt impotent, like a spectator at a tennis match. Watch the ball go back and forth with no input from me. The cases were now in the hands of the NYPD, and I don't have jurisdiction.

The next call came in on my cell phone. The number was blocked, but I suspected the identity of the caller.

"Patti, it's Kelly again. We've been watching CNN with Yusuf, and he swears Karen's killer is one of his guards from the log cabin."

"He's sure?"

"Dead sure. He believes it's the same guy who probably assassinated Grigori and the women. Yusuf took advantage of the situation and slipped out the window," Kelly said.

"What are you going to do with this hot information? Tell the NYPD?"

"No. National Security. The director is on the phone with the NYPD commissioner to let both cases die a natural death."

"No way, Kelly. I've got my Irish temper going. Karen and Luis' deaths can be laid at my doorstep. Please shove your national security BS into a place where the sun doesn't shine. I'm not sitting in the back of the bus any longer."

"Patti, you're nuts. This is the real world. No one cares about Luis and Karen. If Karen's slaughter wasn't shown live on CNN, the story would fill a slot on page forty of the *New York Post*. Get real, girl. Stop trying to become Joan of Arc. If you recall, the French turned Joan over to the English, who then burned her at the stake. This is bigger than us. Let it go for the sake of your career, Patti."

I went silent. Kelly was right, but I didn't give a damn.

"Give me the director's phone number, Kelly."

"Are you kidding? I won't even give you the area code."

"All right then, Kelly. I'm not a homicide commander for nothing. I'll find him."

CHAPTER SIXTY-TWO

THE DIRECTOR

July 7

I was surprised when Ginger told me the FBI director was on line six. I wanted to make a pitch, but deep down, I never thought he would take my call.

"My assistant director prepared a dossier on you, Lieutenant. I took your phone call at her insistence. She warned me if I didn't have a chat with you, I may see you scaling the White House fence. Your resume is impressive. I have a pretty good idea of what this call is about. Go ahead, speak your mind," he said.

"It's a simple request, Director. I want back on the Oleg Petrovsky case and several loose ends are in need of buttoning up. Namely, Oleg, Grigori, Karen, Luis Munoz, and the two women in the log cabin were murdered on the orders of an enigmatic guy who parades around on a bicycle. Unless I, or we, track him down soon, more people will be disposed of with bullets to the back of the head. Your concept of national security and mine are not on the same wavelength. I want security for the rest of the targets with bull's-eyes on their backs. A phone call from you to my boss is all I need."

"Lieutenant, we're coming at this from different directions. I see the entire puzzle while you work around the edges of the picture. Your dead Oleg opened a multination criminal case. The matter is so big and sensitive that I've briefed the president on the details. The case is bigger than your commitment to local murders. We're on top of the thing. If, and when, we bring it to a successful conclusion, we'll include your homicide squad in the accolades. In the meantime, I make no more phone calls."

"That's not the way to go, Director. Murder is murder. We have a plaque hanging in the office. Part of it says, 'No greater honor will ever be bestowed on an officer or a more profound duty imposed on him than when he is entrusted with the investigation of the death of a human being'. There's more, but you get my drift."

"Loud and clear, Lieutenant. You're a good salesperson. I think you could sell ice to the Eskimos in winter. Suppose I take off the cuffs. How do we control you? My briefing paper includes words like *headstrong, adventurous, over-confident,* and *larger-than-life.*"

"I'll work hand in hand with supervisory special agent Kelly Twomey from your New York office. We've worked well together since I called her on the day we found Oleg's body."

"I don't want you to work together. Lieutenant McAvoy will have to take orders from Kelly Twomey or there's no deal. And you will check in with her each and every day. I want a full report on your activities. For your information, I know Kelly. We like her and have her pegged as a rising star in the company. Don't do anything to torpedo her career, agreed?"

"Agreed, Director."

"I'll make the calls."

CHAPTER SIXTY-THREE

Make Something Happen

July 8

Pulling my bewildered team together in the conference room, I told them we were back on the case.

"None other than Chief Corcoran delivered the news this morning. He spoke to me like a man who found out his three adult children were fathered by another man. Confused and angry, he said, 'McAvoy, you'll get yours someday. You've backstabbed me from day one of the Petrovsky case. I can't wait until I take you down. Commissioner O'Driscoll has turned you loose again to work with your friends from the FBI. Have a bad day.'"

Sergeant DiGregorio broke the tension. "Corcoran will get his someday. He's a saboteur instead of a supporter. What's the game plan, boss?"

"We have bodies all over the place in multiple jurisdictions. Karen's killer is on video and was identified by Yusuf Al-Muslim as one of the log-cabin guards. Yusuf also thinks the man whacked Grigori and the women found in the woodshed. Behind the scene is a murky character moving about on a bicycle. Seems our bike man is the big cheese, the general pulling all the strings. I'm going to ask Kelly to produce Yusuf and have the fellow spend time with our police sketch artist. I want a composite of the suspect and another of his bicycle, in color. Kevin and Taylor, have that job as soon as I set it up. I want it done ASAP."

I had no time for either questions or delays. I called Kelly to run the request past her.

"Girlfriend," she said, "the director called me directly this morning. My boss nearly fainted with jealousy. I was told to cooperate with you and report your progress to the director's office daily. What the hell did you say to him?"

"I talked cop-to-cop with him. He understood the logic of my argument and here we are. I want Yusuf to sit with my artist and produce two pictures—bike man and his bicycle. Where may I send Kevin Cassidy and Taylor Morgan?"

"Have them go to Twenty-six Federal Plaza. I'll have Yusuf ready for your troops. Composites are a good idea. What are you going to do with them? I would counsel against releasing them to the news media."

"I agree, Kelly. That would only drive the suspect underground. The guy's already running silent and deep. When I get the pictures, I'll spread them among the Long Beach cops. I know most of the cops and bosses. They're on the ball. If bike man is hanging around the city, I'll put my money on the cops."

"High praise. They must have worked well with you on your cases," Kelly said.

"True. They know every alley and place where the bad actors hang out. One time I asked them to produce so-and-so. Within fifteen minutes, in comes so-and-so held up by the back of his neck. The cops knew which side of the factory alley the guy used as a hangout. Besides, Long Beach and Long Branch are the only credible leads to come out of Yusuf's mouth until Karen's murder showed up on CNN."

"Why not focus on Long Branch, New Jersey?"

"Oleg was murdered on Long Island. Yusuf and Ahmed are from Long Island. New Jersey doesn't fit into the equation. We follow the leads like a bloodhound on the hunt. I'll stick with Long Beach."

"Send your team, Patti. I'm looking forward to meeting General Bike Man. We'll be ready for your artist."

CHAPTER SIXTY-FOUR

DELIVERANCE

Kevin and Taylor e-mailed two color composites—mystery man and his Trek. A careful look into the man's face revealed he was extraordinary. Most people don't stand out in a crowd unless they want to be noticed. It was the black cold eyes of a cobra that gave him away. His eyes said, *I have seen too much.* An attempt to blend in was reinforced with a New York Mets baseball cap and a biker's crash helmet. To me, this face projected evil.

"Check out the photo, Frank. Mr. Met could be hired as a Hollywood extra to play in the good cop–bad cop role. He's made to order as the bad cop. When we get him, Metsie will be a hard nut to crack," I said.

"A hardnose," Frank said. "He reminds me of an old detective, a World War Two marine who also saw too much. Same set jaw and craggy face. I wonder how a guy with a mug like this wound up with two radicalized American Muslim holy warriors. Stereotypes aside, General Bike Man is white, European, and has the persona of a cop. Mr. Met has spent time in interrogation rooms as the questioner. God have mercy on those poor souls. I'm sure Mr. Met didn't."

While Frank preached away, I examined the bicycle. As usual, Taylor had included a set of notes from her research into Trek bicycles. In front of me was a photo of a blue-and-white man's bike. According to Taylor, it's an expensive toy, probably costing several thousand dollars.

Designed in Wisconsin but manufactured overseas. Bike aficionados have their own language and gear—a basket is a bike bag; a rear pouch is a trunk for holding spare parts; gloves are padded but fingerless; and the helmet displayed in the photo would set you back two hundred fifty bucks.

I handed the bike and helmet photo to Frank. He pored over the pictures and Taylor's notes.

"I notice the helmet matches the colors of the Trek. It appears to be a variation of the American flag, only this is a white stripe over blue with red on the bottom. It's a tricolor, similar to the French flag. Strange, Mr. Met dresses like he's homeless and drives the Cadillac of bicycles."

We gathered in the conference room for a chat. I had asked Ginger to run off fifty color copies of the composites. The extra copies were for the Long Beach cops, civilian beach patrol and the lifeguards. Kowalsky and Horton were tasked with running down to Long Beach to distribute the flyers. Frank had put together an accompanying description of Homicide South's prime suspect:

WANTED AS A PERSON OF INTEREST

The subject is wanted for questioning in a series of murders in the New York metropolitan area. Subject travels extensively by bicycle as shown in the photograph. He may be wearing beach clothing, an NY Mets baseball cap and/or a multicolored crash helmet, with white, blue, and red stripes. He is to be approached with caution and should be considered armed and dangerous. If anyone makes contact with the subject, do not attempt to take him into custody. Notify the Long Beach Police or the Nassau County Homicide Squad South. Case number is 27-2016 under the name of Detective Robert Kowalsky.

During this, Taylor and Kevin returned to the office. I shook hands and congratulated them for putting the composites together in record speed.

"No problem, boss," Kevin said. "We hit the red grille lights and siren. Taylor and I figured the front office could put the cuffs back on as fast as they unlocked them."

"Heads-up thinking, guys. I'm sending Kowalsky and Horton to Long Beach to spread the photos around. I want to make something happen."

Kowalsky and Horton were heading for the door when Ginger announced, "Lieutenant, Captain Joe Kearney from Long Beach is on line six."

Everyone froze as I picked up the phone.

CHAPTER SIXTY-FIVE

ALLAHU AKBAR

"Joe, Patti here. Been a long time. Good to hear from you. What's up?"

"We got a hit on a stolen-car alarm broadcast by your people back in May."

"What car, Joe?"

"A 2010 Blue BMW registered to Karen Arkady of Fair Lawn, New Jersey."

I whistled into the phone, analyzing the information. Westbury, Glen Cove, the Bronx, Roscoe, and now Long Beach. I had to let Joe Kearney in on some of the details.

"Joe, Karen was murdered yesterday in a New York City subway, allegedly the victim of a pocketbook snatch gone bad. They showed the crime on CNN. Her killing is connected to an open murder of Oleg Petrovsky from last May in Westbury. What led you to her Beemer?"

"It was in the long-term parking zone of the Allegria Hotel. Security nabbed a couple of kids stealing tires. Seems the Beemer has been there since April sixteenth, covered with a tarp."

"Hold on, Joe. I'm putting you on speaker phone. I want my team to hear this."

Running my hand and arm in a circle, the team gathered around to hang on Joe Kearney's words.

"Who parked an expensive Beemer with Jersey plates in the Allegria? Didn't that raise red flags?"

"Not at all. The Allegria caters to a high-end crowd—stockbrokers, investment bankers, attorneys, and the like. It's not unusual to rent out a spot for an expensive car over several months while the owner is on a business trip or whatever. The Beemer was brought in by a young white man in the company of an attractive dark-haired woman. They paid for the first month."

I mouthed to the crew, *Tanya and Grigori.*

"How much?"

"Five hundred dollars a month plus an extra hundred fifty for a tarp."

"Has the same couple been keeping up on the payments?"

"No. The woman meets an old guy on the boardwalk. According to a horny waiter, the guy slips her an envelope, and she pays the concierge."

"Describe the old man."

"About seventy. Travels on a blue-and-white bicycle. Wears either a Mets cap or a crash helmet."

Kowalsky raised his arms in the fashion of a football referee calling a touchdown. We smiled. I raised my thumb.

"Joe, first things first. I'm sending you two photos—one of the bike man and the other of his bike and helmet. We'll want to show them to the waiter. Make my day and tell me the concierge recorded the transactions."

"Sorry. First thing I looked for. CCTV is out of commission. The Allegria's been in and out of bankruptcy proceedings. I suspect the CCTV system was the victim of a cutback."

"Joe, I'm on my way with fifty copies of each photo. Pass the word to your cops that the bike man is to be considered armed and dangerous. We believe he has blood on his hands for at least five murders. A crime-scene van and tow truck will seize the Beemer. Tell your cops to avoid touching the car. Where are the tire thieves?"

"In police headquarters. We were going to contact the owner, but now we know she's dead. We may have to release the thugs. No complainant, you know."

"Understood, Joe. Get names, addresses, photos and most of all prints. We'll be dusting the Beemer inside and out. Prints from the kids will save us time from tracking them down later. I'll see to it the prints go in the elimination file."

"I'm on it, Patti."

"One more thing, Joe. How did the kids have the balls to pull off a caper at the Allegria?"

"Tonight is Long Beach's Fourth of July fireworks show. The city is mobbed with tourists and sightseers. A lot of them have been drinking. You can hardly drive the roads. The crowds spill into the streets. The kids thought they could pull off the heist in all the confusion. Pretty soon, we'll have to close the main bridge to incoming traffic."

"Joe, don't close it to bicycle riders, please."

"Gotcha, Patti. We'll open the barriers for bikes. Can you get to the city by chopper?"

"Yeah, I think so. I'm supposed to get permission, but I'll come up with something. To hell with all bureaucrats."

"Patti," Joe said, "how come they didn't get rid of the Beemer after the murder? The car is leading you directly to them and Long Beach. Sounds like a mistake to me."

"Tradecraft, Joe. If Karen gets her car back without Oleg, she goes straight to the police to report him as a missing person. No car, no Oleg, and no worries until we accidentally stumbled on the dead body."

"Good. I'll set up a landing zone at the hospital's new heliport. We'll meet your team with our cars. See you soon."

I hung up. "*Que sera sera*," I said. What will be will be. *Allahu Akbar*. Saddle up.

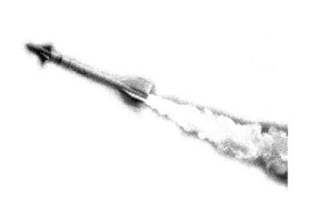

CHAPTER SIXTY-SIX

POSSE

I ran a to-do list through my mind as we sped down Hempstead Turnpike towards the Police Aviation Bureau hangar in the Northrop Grumman complex in Bethpage. The commander, Lieutenant Van Richter, asked, "Do you have a chief's approval for the mission?"

Realizing this could be a career buster, I said, "Van, I left a voice mail with Chief Corcoran. We're on an emergency mission to catch a multiple murderer and maybe prevent a terrorist attack in Long Beach."

Van said, "Patti, whatever Homicide South wants, Homicide South gets. You have six souls for transport? I'll have the Moose warmed up and ready to go."

We arrived in record time and squeezed into the Moose. Running through my to-do list, Kelly got the first call.

"Ever joined a posse, Kelly?"

"Oh Lord, Patti. What's going down? You're like that bunny on television. Patti Mac never stops coming at you. Go ahead, I'm listening."

Five minutes was spent rattling off the details and let Kelly digest the Long Beach story. I could tell Kelly was a good listener and note taker. She neither interrupted nor asked questions until I said, "How long will it take to get Yusuf into the FBI chopper?"

"Jesus, Patti. Now you've gone too far. Producing Yusuf today for composite police sketches is one thing. Having him join your posse is another. In my world, that won't fly, pun intended. My hierarchy would form an exploratory committee and spend three days researching our options. I won't even ask. Why don't you call your new BFF, the director?"

"All right, Kelly. I'll do just that and get back to you."

Hanging up, I heard Kelly plead to not call Washington. "You'll make things difficult. They'll think I put you up to it. No good can come from such a call," she said.

I disregarded her plea and made the call.

"Director's office," a trained voice said.

After giving my name, rank, and serial number, I asked to speak to the director. "I need to talk to him. It's a national security emergency," I said, hoping that would get his attention. It did.

"Lieutenant McAvoy. It's late on a Friday afternoon. You should be sitting in your car heading out east to the Hamptons for a well-deserved weekend off. What's the national-security emergency?" the Director said.

"No time off this weekend, Director." He then got the same five-minute version Kelly was given.

"I need her, the JTTF, and Yusuf Al-Muslim. Only you have the juice to make it happen. Call it an educated guess, but I think something terrible is going to happen in Long Beach."

"Your instincts have been on the money, so far. I'll cover the bet and make the call. Good luck, Lieutenant."

I know I should have felt empathy for Kelly as she was about to take another call from her chairman of the board. She's a sharp woman and knows I'm using her for my own ends. But running a homicide operation is something like a triple play in baseball—bang, bang, bang. No time for second-guessing.

Frank leaned over. "Heard the conversation. Suggestion—flying around Long Beach in the Moose may scare the bad guys off. Since you're twisting arms, how about making a call to Cablevision for their chopper. The fireworks show is a newsworthy event. No one will pay attention to a news media flyover."

"Good idea, Frank. Do it for me while I make a callback to Kelly."

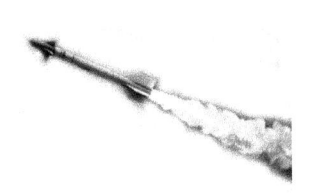

CHAPTER SIXTY-SEVEN

EYE-IN-THE-SKY

Crossing over the Meadowbrook Parkway, the Moose opened a horizon-to-horizon vista of the city of Long Beach. Low-hanging dark clouds surrounded the setting sun. Red taillights strung out along the Loop Parkway like strands of spaghetti testified that tourists were riding the brakes instead of pushing the gas pedals.

"Joe Kearney was right. Our red lights and sirens wouldn't have an effect on the throngs of visitors. We'd be stranded on the Loop Parkway Bridge."

The pilot turned the Moose northwest following Reynolds Channel to the hospital. A fleet of fishing boats for-hire was entering and departing the channel, loaded to the gunwales with amateur fishermen who carried bait and alcohol in their coolers.

Needing dependable backup, I put a call into the Marine Corps of the Nassau County Police Department, the Bureau of Special Operations. Sergeant Bill Connolly, duty officer, answered my call. We had worked together recently while executing the search warrant on Grigori's mail drop in the Bronx.

"Bill, we need backup in Long Beach. It has to do with the murder case in Westbury from last May."

"Yeah, the search-warrant caper. I remember. Where and when do you want us, boss? We're a little light tonight. It's prime vacation time."

I can spare three cops plus yours truly. One of the cops is Kathy Ryan. She's been a player in some of your cases."

"Yeah, I know. That's fine, Bill. Meet me at the Long Beach Headquarters ASAP. We're in the police chopper because traffic is a horror. Free fireworks tonight is bringing them in from far and wide. From the sky, it looks like Mardi Gras and Times Square on New Year's Eve combined."

"No problem, boss. You remember I used to be in the boats. I'll borrow a RHIB and scoot across Reynolds Channel."

"RHIB? That's like a Zodiac, isn't it?"

"Yeah, RHIB stands for Rubber Hull Inflated Boat."

"Thanks, Bill. Bring your heavy weapons. No shooting without a direct order from me."

"Understood, boss. We're moving out now."

Kelly called instead of the other way around. Her voice was cold, to the point, and irritated.

"My assistant director has erupted. Lava is coming out of his ears. He's furious with both of us and swears I put you up to calling Washington. He wants me to find out who you know."

"Kelly, tell him I'm a close friend of Michelle Obama. Your weasel boss should ponder that tidbit for a while and leave you alone."

"Weasel? Wrong word. These guys have misogynist blood embedded in their DNA. Scared, uncertain, and downright afraid simply because the big boss called me directly. Seems our roles have been reversed. You're calling the shots. What's next?"

"Saddle up your JTTF team. Shove them into your largest FBI chopper. Long Beach traffic is in gridlock. Yusuf will be our spotter searching for either the bike man or Tanya and Ahmed. Find one and we've found the nest," I said.

"Where do you want us to land, boss?"

I smarted at the rebuke but pushed on. Bang, bang, bang. Keep the case moving.

"Long Beach rebuilt the hospital after Hurricane Sandy. Have your pilot drop you onto the heliport. Long Beach will meet us with cars."

"Patti, this one is not negotiable. Yusuf is my prisoner. I'm not paroling him to your custody. Yusuf and Finbar will become conjoined twins, handcuffed to each other, and I'll keep the keys. No funny stuff from you. Your old pal Finbar has been instructed to put the bracelets on your wrists. I mean it. Understood?"

I breathed deeply trying to measure the depth of Kelly's anger. This was a side I had not seen.

"Whew, Kelly. I believe you. My motive is to find the Grinch before it does catastrophic damage."

"Indeed, Patti. What a noble quest. If we were in Scotland Yard, the queen could put you on the honors list. Imagine meeting Dame Patricia Ann McAvoy."

"We're not in the U.K., Kelly. I just want the Grinch."

Mollified, Kelly said, "You know we can't fly around in FBI and police choppers. Our markings will give us away. The people we're looking for are cunning. We'll get made after the first sweep."

"Working on it, Kelly. Trying to commandeer Cablevision's eye-in-the-sky. The bad guys won't pay attention to a news-media chopper."

"Pretty cunning yourself, Patti. See you."

CHAPTER SIXTY-EIGHT

Party Crashers

Good thing I had charged my phone battery in the morning. Joe Kearney was on the line. His voice let on there was a problem.

"Patti, tell your pilot to abort the landing at the hospital. Land your machine in the Lido Beach Golf Course parking lot near the city border. I've cleared the place out for you."

"Why, Joe?"

"My guys went to meet you and came across a strange, unmarked black helicopter parked on the pad. Two sinister dudes were hanging around. When the ER nurse spotted my guys, she told them the copter had no business in her space, landed without approval. She thought it belonged to arrogant rich businessmen pushing their weight around for the fireworks show to avoid traffic. My cops thought otherwise. The characters had the swagger of mercenaries. They tried to make calls, but we grabbed the phones."

"Joe, who are they? What do they have to say?"

"That's the rub, Patti. Guttural heavy accents and shrugs. Claim to speak no English. We separated the pair, cuffed them, and tossed them into the backseats of police cars. A quick frisk and up pops two fully loaded forty-caliber Glocks with the serial numbers filed down. And get this—each is carrying a Russian passport. Are these guys connected to the bike man?"

"For sure, Joe. Our murder victim, Oleg Petrovsky, was a Russian national on the payroll of the Federal Security Service, the equivalent of our FBI. The Beemer you found belonged to Oleg's girlfriend."

"Wow. From Russia with Love. What a story. This is a bad bunch. No sign of the pilot. If he shows, we'll pounce on him."

"Good job, Joe. Hold the Russians where they are. I have someone in the FBI chopper who may identify them as players in Oleg's murder."

"OK. I've sent two vans to pick up your teams."

"Can you spare a third? Four BSO cops are coming to help us out. They're crossing Reynolds Channel in a Zodiac type of boat. I'm told they'll hit the beach on the northern side of the course. Grounds crews have been dispatched with golf carts to play taxi."

"Patti, the operation has the tempo of a D-Day invasion. Any other surprises?"

"Yeah. I'm going to grab Cablevision's news copter. Is there room at the golf course parking lot for another whirlybird?"

"I'll make room. Just don't try to land Air Force One. We don't have the space."

I laughed for a second as I hung up and called Kelly.

"The Russians have landed," I said.

The story of the black helicopter, Glocks, and mercenary types didn't phase Kelly—Russian passports got her going. I passed on the new landing-zone directions. "Yusuf is going to take a gander at the prisoners after your helicopter lands."

"The director is either going to kiss you or have you sent incognito to the Witness Protection Program. Bike man has set himself to get out of Dodge City fast. Wonder why? The goddamned Grinch is primed for action. If I was him, my crosshairs would be aimed at a spectacular target."

I slapped the palm of my hand against my forehead.

"Kennedy Airport is down the road, Kelly. Jesus, why didn't I think of it? They were going to hit a plane at LaGuardia. Why not Kennedy?

Another target-rich environment. I was distracted by the fireworks show. Thought they'd try to blow up the barge and kill a bunch of civilians. It's a passenger plane they're after."

Silence.

"Your argument is on the money, Patti. Our wheels will be down in five minutes. I can see you and a news copter circling for landing. We've got a lot to do. How do we shut down one of the world's largest airports on a gut feeling?"

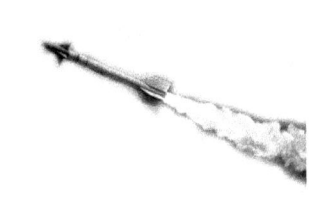

CHAPTER SIXTY-NINE

COMBINED OPERATIONS

"Kelly, your credentials have much more clout than my little gold badge. After landing, you have the job of diverting all aircraft coming out of JFK. At the very least, have the planes avoid Long Island's south shore. I'll leave the salesmanship to your Irish charm."

"Anything else, Chief?" Kelly said with the bite of a woman who knows she's being used and can't do a thing about it.

"Yes," I said. "Finbar, Taylor, and Kevin will take Yusuf for a show up. Two Russians are on ice at the hospital. Yusuf may make our day. His presence might scare them into saying something."

Kelly was irate. "If I don't follow your orders, Chief, how will you rat me out to the director? He's probably gone home for the weekend."

"No problem," I retorted. "He gave me his private cell-phone number. I won't have to use it, will I?"

Silence.

The kind of silence at a poker game when the guy holding three aces can't figure out if his opponent is bluffing.

"All right, Chief McAvoy. I'll go along for now, but Finbar stays with Yusuf."

I won the battle, but the rest of the war was yet to be played out as the Moose touched down on the golf course, followed by Cablevision and the FBI. As promised, Joe Kearney met us with vans and unmarked police cars. Piling out of a van, Bill Connolly and his BSO cops joined us.

The grounds crew gawked at the choppers, men and women in suits, and pilots in jumpsuits. When the BSO cops emerged in black SWAT-type outfits carrying Heckler & Koch automatic rifles, the crew backed off. One shouted, "I know about those guns. They're ballistic jackhammers. Those cops ain't here for no crowd control."

Cars and vans whisked away Kelly and Joe Kearney to police headquarters. Finbar's team made for the hospital parking lot for a rendezvous with the Russians, backed up by Sergeant Connelly and his BSO crew.

"The die is cast," I said to Frank. "How did you get Cablevision to give up the chopper?"

"Words like *national security* and *police emergency* can work even on jaded news characters. You owe a big thanks to Shelby Lynde. She opened the right doors for me. The pilot is gung ho and ready to help. I took the liberty of assigning Finbar and the others, including Yusuf, to search the crowd from Cablevision's chopper."

"Frank, you bring new meaning to the expression eye-in-the-sky. I like it when you go the extra yard to make something happen. This is a big challenge."

"Yeah, boss. Something like eating an elephant, one piece at a time."

For the first time, I enjoyed a real belly laugh.

"Frank, when you retire, write a book of quotations. It'll be a best seller."

Kevin's callback number lit up my phone.

"Boss, Yusuf identified both characters as guards from the log cabin. He claims they forced the victims into the woodshed but didn't do any shooting. Yusuf suspected all along they weren't real Muslims as they prayed together."

"Why, Kevin?"

"The Russians went through the motions. None of them touched their forehead to the floor. They played a role to convince our radicalized Muslim he was in devout company. It finally dawned on Yusuf he's been manipulated by a gang of clever Russian thugs. I deputized him. Yusuf's a sworn member of our posse."

"Did Yusuf scare them into talking to Kevin?"

"Yeah. Started out with the usual,' We were following orders.' Turns out they're ex- *Spetsnaz* soldiers, toughest sons of bitches in Russia. Something like our Navy SEALS. They realized federal prison is their destiny. According to the weaker of the two, the man in charge made his bones with the KGB and still holds the rank of general. Everyone is terrified of the guy."

"That would be the bike man?"

"Yeah. Finbar's colleagues are debriefing them as we speak."

"Good work, Kevin. Hold on a second, I have Joe Kearney on my line."

"Patti, get your choppers in the air. Bike man just crossed the Long Beach Bridge heading south toward Park Avenue. He's decked out in full regalia—multi-colored white, blue, and red helmet, white tape wrapped around the handlebars for traction, and his bike has flashing lights, front and rear. The guy is lit up like the Fire Island lighthouse. I have two bicycle cops trailing him at a safe distance. Should be easy for your crew to track him by air."

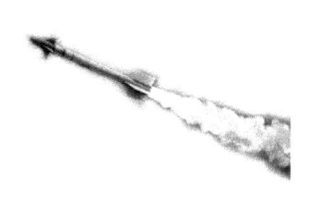

CHAPTER SEVENTY

Follow that Bike

"The general has come out of hiding," I said to Frank. "He's slipped across the bridge on his bike sticking to Long Beach Boulevard. The road slopes toward the ocean. General what's-his-name is coasting along without a care. Two Long Beach bicycle patrol cops are stalking him from a distance. All we need to make their job easier is to paint the Russian flag on the back of his shirt."

"It's practically on his back, boss," Taylor said as she unloaded from a van with Yusuf, Finbar, and Kevin.

"How so, Miss Researcher?"

"When the Russians got rid of the hammer and sickle flag, it was replaced with a tricolor composed of three bright stripes—snow white over royal blue with fire engine red on the bottom."

"Damn him," I said, "the general has been taunting us by displaying the Russian colors in a subliminal manner. I want to meet this boy."

A convoy of cars and vans poured into the Lido's parking lot. I handed out job assignments. Cablevision had priority as the most important to get airborne. I grabbed Yusuf, still shackled to Finbar's wrist.

"Listen to me, radical boy. Do exactly what this agent wants or by God, I'll take you up, fly over the fireworks barge, and accidentally drop you into a mortar tube. You'll arrive in paradise as seventy-two chunks of beef, one for each virgin," I said.

Finbar picked up the act like an extra reading his lines.

"That's right, Yusuf," Finbar said, "take the lieutenant at her word. She's capable of doing something like that."

Yusuf nodded. He had found himself surrounded by so many crazies in the last few months, he assumed I was another loose cannon.

"I'll give you no trouble, Lieutenant. My eyes will be peeled for Ahmed. I assume wherever this general goes, Ahmed won't be far away."

I nodded. "Get it done, Yusuf."

"All right, Pilot. Wheels up. The prime suspect is traveling by bike on Long Beach Boulevard. We'll take to the air and stay a respectable distance. Let your passenger find him, you navigate the chopper."

"I'll help out. I know this city from flyovers after Hurricane Sandy. For your information, part of my job is evaluating the weather. Those thick gray clouds are called nimbostratus. We're in for a downpour in maybe an hour, give or take."

"Then get moving," I said. "Heavy rain and fireworks don't mix. Showtime may be cancelled, and we lose our target in the melting crowds."

As Cablevision's chopper lifted and flew westbound, Kelly arrived in a speeding Long Beach police car.

She said, "Kearney filled me in on the general. I've got the FAA, CIA, FBI, and God knows who else outraged. Reluctantly, the FAA will divert outbound aircraft by way of New Jersey with approval to hook east to Europe and Africa. By the time they gain altitude, they'll be far enough out to sea to avoid the Grinch. Inbound flights are cleared to land by way of Long Island's North Shore. It's amazing how fast they cut the orders, but they left no doubt that my ass is on the line. Where's Finbar?"

"Playing eye-in-the-sky with Yusuf and my guys," I said.

Kelly glanced and watched as the pilot dipped the chopper's nose, clipping along toward the city center.

"Kelly, you go up with Frank and two BSO cops. Your JTTF troops have to stay with the Russian prisoners and squeeze them for every drop of information. Have your pilot hover over the east end of the city. I'm in the Moose with Ron, Bob, and two BSO cops, Bill Connolly and Kathy Ryan. We'll circle around the west end."

"Is that all, Chief McAvoy?"

"Aw, knock it off, Kelly. It's getting old. We've no room for spectators at this show. Everyone is locked and loaded. Someone has to make things happen. That someone happens to be me."

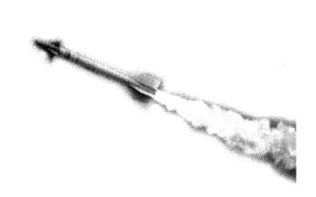

CHAPTER SEVENTY-ONE

SNAFU

"Uh-oh," Taylor announced over the walkie-talkie radio.

"What's up, Taylor?"

"Looks like we've got a problem, boss. General Biker hit the brakes, skidded to a stop to get into a shouting match with a guy standing alone at the foot of the boulevard and the boardwalk."

"Describe him."

"White, forties, dressed in the same dark outfit as the guys from the helicopter except for gold wings over his heart. Pilot is my best guess. The chat is getting lively. General Biker jumped off his machine and is going nose to nose with the pilot. Wagging his finger, the general is behaving like a man who would like to have a hammer in his hand to use on a subordinate. Pilot man is standing, hands at his sides, taking it."

"I wish you could read lips, Taylor. I'd give up my vacation to hear the conversation."

"Look out. General just shoved his pilot and is pointing up Long Beach Boulevard. I suspect our strange visitor abandoned his helicopter to go sightseeing, got caught by the principal playing hooky, and is getting one hell of an ass chewing. There he goes, jogging north toward Park Avenue, probably to the hospital and his helicopter."

I switched the call channel to talk to the FBI chopper.

"Kelly, you got that?"

"Loud and clear. We'll make a loop around and take up a position near the hospital."

"Good. Find a spot for the BSO cops to intercept the pilot. He's to be considered armed and dangerous. I'll get backup from the Long Beach cops."

Joe Kearney jumped into the discussion.

"Patti, I've been listening. There's a strip mall not far from the hospital. Your pilot will have to pass it, turn up a side street, and make his way to the heliport. Drop your guys into the back of the mall. I'll have backup waiting. The cops can pounce on the guy like hungry cats on a mouse."

"Good plan, Joe. I want the pilot out of action before he has a chance to call the general. I'll check in with Kelly and Taylor."

"Speaking of the general, Taylor, what's he doing now?"

"Sitting on the bike, eyeballing his pilot scooting up the road back to his abandoned post. I think Mr. Pilot will soon be joining Grigori and the rest."

"Why?"

"General's face reads like a man who has just passed a sentence of death on his wayward subordinate. For your information, Yusuf has positively identified the general as *El Supremo* who was in the heated argument with Grigori at the cabin."

"Be patient everyone. General Biker Man is flying into my spiderweb. I'm going to swoop down on him and nail the bastard."

My cop pilot had bad news for me.

"Better give your spiderweb an umbrella, Lieutenant. Raindrops are hitting the windshield. I may have to put the Moose down until the storm passes. Sorry, but that's one rule even I can't bend."

The news and the sadness on my pilot's face hit me like a nightstick across the head.

"OK, I get it."

Hoping for a ray of sunshine in this mess I called the Cablevision copter.

"Taylor, any movement?"

"Yeah. Raindrops on his helmet broke the general's trance. Trying to navigate the boardwalk was a no-go. The crowds are too thick. He's made a quick U-turn onto Shore Road, heading east. Shore runs parallel to the boardwalk.

"Any chance he's spotted your crew stalking him?"

"Nah. He's so pissed off at his pilot, his eyes aren't on us at all. General Biker is behaving like a sergeant who found a soldier sleeping on guard duty—so focused on the soldier, he missed an enemy patrol creeping up on him."

Kelly jumped into the banter.

"BSO and Long Beach cops are inside a mall back alley. A block away, the jogger is shuffling along, getting a little winded. His boss must have scared the hell out of him. Pilot man is getting close, arms drooping, huffing, and puffing."

I waited. Waiting is the terrible cross police commanders carry. Waiting for others to pull off the arrest. Waiting for something to go wrong. I didn't have to wait long.

"Kelly here. They got him. He's on the ground in cuffs. There was no fight left in him. A search of the prisoner turned up a loaded handgun and a cell phone. Long Beach and BSO are taking him into headquarters."

"That's a relief, Kelly. Cablevision's still on the general. I'm told he just turned onto Lincoln Boulevard heading toward the boardwalk where he paused to look around the streets. He neglected to look up. Seeing nothing suspicious, he rode up to the main entrance of the Aqua."

"Break, break," Taylor said, cutting off my conversation. "General in charge of killing is being greeted by a security guard, a clone of all the others we've snatched up today. We've found the nest."

CHAPTER SEVENTY-TWO

Penthouse

Screw the rain. I pushed the Moose pilot to get a view of the Aqua.
"C'mon, we're close. General put himself inside the place to finalize the carnage. He can't see us for the next minute or so."

"OK, Lieutenant. As you know, I learned how to fly this kite from my years in Iraq and Afghanistan. I know firsthand what these bastards will do. I'll push the envelope for you."

"Tell your boss I ordered you to stay in the air."

"Not a chance. I'm the captain of this ship. It's my call and responsibility. But thanks anyway for trying to watch my back."

Joe Kearney lit up my cell phone.

"Patti, I didn't want to talk on the radio, The Aqua is new to the neighborhood, finished up just before Sandy hit Long Beach. Aqua has all the bells and whistles of a high-end residence. Preconstruction prices started at six figures. Private elevators, twenty-four-seven security, inside pool, and a personal beach area are part of the amenities. Here's the bad news."

"Go ahead, Joe."

"Top floor is a penthouse unit with an open patio half the size of a football field. A wet bar from the Plaza Hotel found its way to the roof along with several barbecue pits. Perfect vantage point for a Grinch launch. To make matters worse, Aqua has erected weather-resistant tents and an arbor, decorated with hanging plants. Usually, a crowd of guests are invited to watch the fireworks display. Have someone eyeball the patio. No crowd means nothing good is about to happen."

"I see the penthouse. No party on the roof tonight, Joe."

"One more thing to put in the back of your mind."

"Let's have it, Joe."

"Cookie Weinstein, an institution among real-estate brokers, sold several Aqua units recently. Cookie's a missing person. I don't know if it's a coincidence."

"Joe, there are no coincidences in a murder case. We'll have to put Cookie on the back burner for now. Tell me more about the Aqua."

"Biggest problem for you is the network of underground parking. Steel-gated entry is complemented by an exit gate on Shore Road. I'm preparing several vans and city garbage trucks for a roadblock. Shore Road will become a bottleneck if they decide to get into the wind and make a run for the helicopter. By the way, we disabled the engine. The thing won't get much airtime."

"Joe, win, lose, or draw. You're my guest at Jordan's Lobster House. Long Beach certainly gets its money's worth out of you. How's it going with the *Spetsnaz* prisoners?"

"The JTTF guys are pros. Classic criminal investigators. The bad guys are sitting in separate rooms undergoing interrogation. Their eyes have the stare of hopeless men who know they're swimming in a bottomless lake. Sooner or later, they'll tire and give it up. You know, it's not the illegal acts that have them worried. Getting caught, losing the chopper has them terrified. Your general fellow has them scared to death. He's an ominous guy and needs to be taken out of circulation."

Kelly's callback number interrupted us. She hit me with a thunderbolt.

"Patti, I've run this scenario round and round through my mind, trying to connect the dots. Swirling about are the Russians, ISIS, radicalized Americans, and stolen Russian army Grinches. We've documented the theft of many Grinches from a Russian airbase in Syria. My dilemma is putting an answer to this question. How did rockets glommed by ISIS terrorists wind up back in Russian hands to be used in the American homeland?"

"I'm following, Kelly. Continue."

"Russia lied about the number of missing Grinches. There were just enough stolen to provide a grain of truth to the reports. Several were smuggled into America for Ahmed and Yusuf to play with and point the finger of blame at ISIS."

"What does Russia get out of this?"

"American outrage, followed by war with ISIS. Behind our back, Russia gets time to bolster the Assad regime in Syria. Iraq, Iran, Libya, and oil rich countries will allow Russia to emerge as the real caliphate, leaving us to murder every ISIS member."

"Your dissertation is good enough for a doctoral thesis, Kelly. I can't find a flaw in your argument. We've got to stop the general at all costs."

Loudspeakers along the boardwalk announced the cancellation of the fireworks display. A loud groan, some cursing, and flipping of the bird at the speakers followed. The cancellation had an unexpected result.

"Taylor here, boss. I see a bearded young man running amok on the penthouse roof, ranting and raving, punching his fists into the air. A dark-haired woman is trying to calm him down. Yusuf says, that's Ahmed and Tanya."

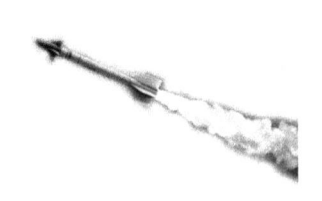

CHAPTER SEVENTY-THREE
HOT LANDING ZONE

Damn. The cancellation pressed hard on Ahmed's over-the-edge button. I picked up the radio to order an all-out assault when Joe Kearney broke in.

"Patti, I sent a pair of undercover detectives to the Aqua, under the scam of wanting to use their bathroom. My guys aren't far from the Aqua on pickpocket, drunk, and fight patrol. Unless you say stop, my guys have orders to take down the guards while you deal with the mess on the roof. The men tell me there are two guards."

"Go."

Before I collected my thoughts on the assault, Taylor interrupted.

"Boss, Ahmed's gone ballistic. I've seen men go off the charts, and he's in the crazy range. He'd laugh off a dozen Taser shots and rip your head off. He's gone over the edge. Just threw Tanya at the penthouse parapet so hard, she's lying unconscious. She smacked her head hard. Swear he's going to throw her off the roof."

"We don't need that. I want her alive."

"Hold on. Here comes the cavalry. Our general must have heard the noise and came to break up the fight, gun in hand."

"Is he shooting?"

"No. He's frozen in a classic combat stance, both hands on the gun. Looks afraid to kill his assassin. No one left to fire the Grinch. General switched his gun to the left hand and flung his crash helmet at Ahmed. It hit him, but he pushed it aside. The men are staring at each other. Tanya's lying in a bloody heap by the parapet."

"What now?"

"General still has his gun trained on Ahmed. He's pulled a cell phone from his pocket and is shouting into it. Now he's shaking it to make it work. That accomplished nothing, so he tossed it."

"No one will answer. Long Beach cops nailed the lobby security guards. General has no backup."

I got back to the immediate problem.

"All units. Converge on the target. Anyone with a clear shot has my approval to go ahead. Don't waste time asking for permission. We have to take out these guys before they add more innocent victims to their head count. It's kill or be killed. No need to acknowledge my order."

Cassidy aboard the Cablevision copter jumped in.

"Ahmed spit at the general, then ducked behind the arbor. All those hanging plants are blocking our view."

"Stay on him, Kevin. I'm coming in from the west. FBI is flying in from the east. What's Ahmed doing now?"

"Jesus, boss. He's coming out of hiding and spotted our copter and Yusuf. He pointed his middle finger at us, then ran back to the arbor. The general finally saw what Ahmed saw and fired a volley of rounds at us. No harm done. Bit too far for a handgun. General needs to go back to the Russian pistol range. Our pilot is no slouch. He saw it coming and dropped us like a stone. We're back on them."

"I'm up the road from you. Got a clear view of the roof. Reminds me of movies about Vietnam, hot landing zones and all that."

"Ahmed's back, boss, carrying a long green tube. Must be the Grinch. He's trying to insert a shiny silver object down the barrel. Damn thing is a giant hypodermic needle."

"Far worse, Kevin. It's a rocket, and Ahmed is going to use it on one of us."

"Right. Ahmed is nervous. Forgot to pop a rubber gasket protecting the barrel."

"Let's get him while he's fumbling around. You take out the general. We have a better angle for a kill shot on Ahmed. If we miss, our rounds will fall into the sea. Don't miss, Kevin."

"I won't. The bastard has fled the battlefield. For an old guy, he moves like a cheetah."

"No problem, Kevin. Long Beach cops will nail him. They've got a phalanx of cops around the building."

I slid over to make room for the BSO cops. Kathy Ryan was closest to the door.

"Make sure, Kathy. Stick it to him."

Ryan buried the butt of her Heckler & Koch into her shoulder, clicked off the fire-safety switch, and took aim. She ran into trouble. A helicopter in a rainstorm is like a ship at sea, subject to turbulent winds. Weather plays havoc with the best shooter's line of sight. Then we got lucky. Ahmed appeared confused by multiple cop-packed helicopters coming to kill him. He had one shot for one kill and didn't react quickly. A fusillade of bullets flew from Ryan's weapon and found the target. Ahmed was split apart. His torso flew into the arbor; his legs fell to the floor. The infamous Grinch had made its way from Syria to Long Beach to wind up unfired on a luxurious penthouse roof alongside the shooter's legs. I instructed the Moose pilot to land us next to the Grinch.

"Bob, take charge of Tanya. Now you may mark the case closed with an arrest."

"Thanks, boss," Bob said unable to smother an ear-to-ear smile. Horton and Kowalsky ran to handcuff a bewildered Tanya who found herself staring into the business end of Kowalsky's .40 caliber Glock.

"All units," I broadcast. "Land on the beach and meet me at the penthouse."

Cablevision and the FBI choppers veered off to land on an empty beach. A few leftover tourists on the boardwalk had front-row seats to a historical event. They didn't understand the event but cheered. They knew enough to realize an air battle had ended in victory for the good guys.

Joe Kearney made my day.

"We got your general trying to float past a roadblock on his bicycle. He nearly collapsed when a half-dozen cops pointed weapons at him. True to form, he demanded the reason for his arrest."

"What did you charge him with, Joe?"

"Violation of a city ordinance prohibiting operating a bicycle without a helmet. He didn't get the humor."

"Very few people understand cop humor, Joe. We live in our own world."

"That's true. We searched the general and found a Glock minus bullets. He emptied the magazine at your copter. There's one more thing, Patti."

"No more Russian prisoners. We've run out of room keeping them separated."

"OK. We've taken Miss Tanya into custody She's heading for an interrogation room in Homicide South. Thanks for all your help. Long Beach should be proud of its police department."

Kelly Anne Twomey stepped out of the private penthouse elevator. Looking over the carnage—Ahmed split in two, an immobile Grinch, and Tanya in handcuffs—she came over to me and extended her right hand.

"Sorry for being a pain in the neck, Patti. I know I stand in the shadow of a better woman."

ADDENDUM

Russian Revenge-The Hoax at the Aqua is a fictionalized story based on actual meetings in the Aqua Condominium of Long Beach, New York, during the summer of 2015.

On June 30, a local real-estate broker approached the Aqua board representing her client—a well-dressed, articulate young man, allegedly speaking for his father, one of Russian President Vladimir Putin's oligarchs.

Over a three-month period, the board spent time on due diligence and taking the matter seriously. The board wanted to ensure the protection of "the Aqua family."

Hours were spent reviewing the potential buyer's security request for bulletproof windows, titanium floors and wall coverings, upgraded high-speed security elevators, and the introduction of Russian army–trained *Spetsnaz* security guards throughout the building.

The board discovered similar "secure buildings" did exist, the most prominent being located at One Hyde Park in London.

The Aqua is a condominium, not a co-op. The board took the matter seriously as it has little control over potential sales. Therefore, the board spent many hours meeting with the "buyer's" son, who arrived on numerous occasions, tethered to an attaché case containing what he alluded to as confidential files. The buyer was often accompanied to the Aqua by his own team of bodyguards.

A bombshell development occurred on September 17. The Aqua board president received a forty-three-minute phone call, purportedly from the FBI. The president was directed to cancel all further contact with the Russian buyer. According to the FBI, the man was a dangerous arms dealer covered with diplomatic immunity. The FBI caller stated the bureau was attempting to "contain the subject within the confines of Manhattan."

Shortly thereafter, the board was notified that the "Russian buyer" was withdrawing his purchase offer and terminating all further communications.

The board never discovered the true nature of the bizarre request. In retrospect, the board determined the entire episode was indeed a hoax, perpetrated by a delusional young man, the true purpose of which will probably never be discovered.

Numerous members of the Aqua board encouraged the writing of this novel, memorializing the episode for the condominium's historical record. The encouragement has given rise to *Russian Revenge*, a purely fictional account of what may have been the underlying reason for the proposed multiple-unit purchases.

In the time frame of current world chaos, the resulting novel seems not only possible but plausible as well. It offers the reader an insider view of current law-enforcement practices used to protect the American public from international terrorism.

BDS JFN

ACKNOWLEDGEMENTS

Gratitude to the Aqua Condominium Board of Managers for allowing us to memorialize, in a fictionalized manner, a hoax that was perpetrated upon the Aqua in the summer of 2015.

Heartfelt thanks to Inspector Henry Hack, Nassau County Police Department (retired) for his invaluable reading of *Russian Revenge* and offering constructive comments. Henry is the author of seven crime novels.

Likewise, Rita Kushner pored over the manuscript and made many grammar and punctuation suggestions.

A tip of the hat to Howard Stables, a bicycle aficionado, who provided the authors with his expert knowledge.

Many thanks to Dr. Lev Lubarsky, who helped the authors with Russian phrases and expressions.

A big round of applause to the famous Terrorist Cop, Mordecai Dzikansky, a retired First-Grade New York City Police Detective who provided invaluable assistance to allow us to get inside the mind of terrorists.

Finally, no novel is ever complete without the input of a capable copyeditor. Adriana Lubarsky devoted time and attention to detail while reviewing the manuscript. Her efforts improved the flow of the story line while contributing to a good story.

CPSIA information can be obtained
at www.ICGtesting.com
Printed in the USA
LVHW04s1424090918
589613LV00001B/290/P